FAILURE TO THRIVE
A NOVEL

JEFF OLIVER

FAILURE TO THRIVE
A NOVEL

LIVRES **DC** BOOKS

Cover illustration   by Virginie Egger.
Author photograph by Jeremy Kohm.
Book designed and typeset by Primeau Barey, Montreal.
Edited by David McGimpsey.

Library and Archives Canada Cataloguing in Publication
Oliver, Jeff, 1975-
Failure to thrive/Jeff Oliver.
ISBN 978-1-897190-75-3 (pbk.).
ISBN 978-1-897190-76-0 (bound)
1. Title.
PS8629.L574F34 2011   C813'.6   C2011-906654-8

For our publishing activities, DC Books gratefully acknowledges the financial
support of the Canada Council for the Arts, of SODEC, and of the Government
of Canada through the Book Publishing Industry Development Program (BPIDP).

Canada Council   Conseil des Arts
for the Arts   du Canada

Société
de développement
des entreprises
culturelles
Québec ✚ ✚
         ✚ ✚

Printed and bound in Canada by Groupe Transcontinental.
Interior pages printed on FSC® certified environmentally responsible paper.
Distributed by LitDistCo.

MIX
Paper from
responsible sources
FSC
www.fsc.org   FSC® C011825

DC Books
PO Box 666, Station Saint-Laurent
Montreal, Quebec H4L 4V9
www.dcbooks.ca

To my dear, sweet wife Liz.

ACKNOWLEDGEMENTS

I'd owe a great debt of gratitude to the good people at DC Books for making this happen: Steve Luxton, Keith Henderson, and Angela Leuck. A very special thanks to my editor, David McGimpsey, whose feedback and encouragement were invaluable. Also, big thanks to Jon Paul Fiorentino, who championed this book early on.

Thanks to early editors of this text: Analee Stein, Joe Oliver, David Oliver, and Liz Blazer.

Thanks to all the people who have supported my writing over the years. For their inspiration, advice and creative nudges: Greg Ames, Chloe Plaunt, Nancy Foley, Kevin Lee, Bonita Blazer, Tim Hedberg, Elizabeth Dorosin, David K. Israel, Noam Muscovitch, Birgit and Adam Weiner, Jeremy Kohm, David Bell, Kerry Krouse, Marc Golden, Carey Harrison, Maureen Medved, Michael Cunningham, Devon Williams, Molly O'Rourke, G. Hamilton Braithwaite, Bradley Damsgaard, Ayla Teitelbaum, Jeannie Mai, Colin and Yael Stein, Yankee Pot Roast, and my Brooklyn College MFA Class.

Thanks to my Food Network family for all your support and best wishes. Special thanks to Allison Page, Bob Tuschman, Bill Kossman, Brian Lando, Kristin Glick, Chris Castelonia, James Manzi, and Zaire Saunders.

And finally thanks to my son Evan Oliver, who kept me up all night for months, affording me valuable time to write this book.

FOREWORD TO *FAILURE TO THRIVE,* POEMS BY ELLIOT FARB

By The Author's Father

Dear Reader,

The book of poems you are about to read marks the arrival of a gifted new writer to the literary scene. His voice, as you will quickly discover in this debut collection, glimmers with raw energy, imagination, and a sense of Salingeresque alienation that may well define his generation. The author, whom I am also proud to call my son, has achieved something grand between these covers and deserves the highest acclaim. But this book represents so much more than just the early poetic renderings of a young scribe. It is about hard work; it is about diligence; but mainly it is about an intense mental anguish and near-Ghandian suffering endured by a mostly silent benefactor without whose generous eleemosynary relief this book would not exist. Namely me.

Yes, while the ensuing pages may appear as merely a collection of poems, it can best be described as the fruits of twelve years' labor in the field of reality television production and six in the highly competitive but equally lucrative field of series development, during which the author's father (and sole supporter) bankrolled the quixotic whims of his prodigal son (the esteemed author) while said author, if my AmEx bill is any indication, whiled away his days in bohemian rapture sipping Chai tea lattes in trendy cafés and scribbling outrageous socialist platitudes in leather-bound notebooks. Actualized budgets! Product integration! Syndication residuals! These are concepts about which the author remains so blissfully unaware, yet from which he continues to benefit as they fill the proverbial ink in his shiny new proverbial iPad.

Suffice it is to say I should have cut him off years ago. Then he'd be a lawyer! Or work in Institution Sales like that Eli Feldman kid. TD Bank already made him a Vice President–at twenty-five! He's getting married in the fall, too. A real piece of ass I hear–and from a rich family! I mean, Jesus Christ, Elliot just take your goddamned GMATs! I'll pay! An MBA can only help you in life even if you do seem determined to spend it as a moral reprobate.

But I digress. My point is that being a starving artist isn't free anymore. Even Jack Kerouac had to hit the old man up for some coin once in a while. And when Kerouac penned *On the Road* in 1958, coffee cost a nickel. For a quarter you could get a three-course meal, a place to stay, and a date with the farmer's daughter. Not so these days. Ask the wrong person to half-caff your latt-frapp and you could be out six bucks! And so it was with an informed hesitation that I accepted the offer to pen this Foreword: "About time!" I exclaimed into the receiver of a collect call, "Finally some recognition!" Not only for my years of indentured servitude but as thanks for genetic gifts bestowed (the apple doesn't fall far from the tree and as a star contributor to *The McGill Tribune* these "apples" were self-evident). But as I hung up the phone my momentary contentment at finally being acknowledged was clouded by a nagging doubt which loomed like the sword of Damocles over my head in the form of a question: How much is this shit gonna cost me? Am I in for another four years of highway robbery, frustratedly paying bills that chart my son's daily life as he moves from anti-World Bank demonstration (T-shirt, $18), to sushi lunch at Niku ($56), and beers at the Snake Pit ($40), then finally to a late-night drug-store run ($9) where he almost certainly bought rubbers to service the nubile young Betty that would join him for a night of screwing in his overpriced Annex apartment ($1,850/month)? CDs! DVDs! DSL! TiVo! Not to mention the slew of "cash advances" that facilitate the purchase of what I can only conclude is reefer given my son's complete lack of ambition to find a real job or for that matter a decent wife who might someday provide me with a grandson? It's slow-motion patricide!

So, Dear Reader, I give to you the simple budget below. It accounts for the costs of a slim volume of poetry borne by me, the exploited, oft-naïve and endlessly generous Papa. The budget is by no means exhaustive. It accounts for only the two years during which this book was produced and I have omitted rent and food, which I also begrudgingly provided. I have also left out such less tangible but steep costs as sleep deprivation, hair loss, and ceaseless mental torment as I watched my son, the hope of my genetic future, ignore my good guidance and make a flurry of exquisitely poor choices that will surely lead him (and possibly me!) to a life of misery and penury. There can be no price tag on such things, yet the cost is oh so high.

So enjoy the budget! And of course the collection. With the exception of a startlingly byzantine poem on page 13 which engenders some of the moral relativism and politically correct angst whose influence I can only attribute to his mother, it's a darn good read. But in that there should be little surprise. The author is after all my son. I'm proud of who he has become—and I love him with every beat of my heart.

Yours truly,

Jonathan Farb

A FISCAL BUDGET FOR THE PUBLICATION
OF *FAILURE TO THRIVE*
Tabulated by the Poet's Father

DESCRIPTION	COST
MacBook Pro (fully loaded)	$1,300
"Vintage" typewriter	$280
Sensa pens	$320
Leather-bound notebooks (from Italy)	$150
Gauloise cigarettes (rolled pouches imported from France)	$600
Soy lattes	$380
Nehru Jackets	$500
Super 8 camera (reconditioned)	$400
Print pornography	$175
A summer doing "community theatre" in Prague	$9,000
DVD pornography	$83
Useless art degree	$57,500
Kill Whitey: An Anthology of Black Radicalism	$48
Harmonica lessons	$500
Vespa motor scooter (mint green)	$678
U.S. Travel Health Insurance (that I told him to get)	$0

U.S. Emergency medical expenses when he broke
  his arm playing basketball in Chicago with no insurance. $5,900
Internet pornography $120
Legal fees in the case of Elliot Farb v. milf-maestro.com
  (whose $1.99 offer for "hot M.I.L.F.-on-M.I.L.F. action"
  turned into a six thousand dollar Tijuana spending
  bonanza on my credit card.) $15,000
Therapy (130 hours on "Why Daddy ruined me" with a
  cardigan-wearing wackjob named "Dr. Miguel") $16,000
Bail $1,200
Vintage T-shirts $330
D.J. turntables (never used) $450
"Full Release" work from illegal immigrants working
  at Chin-Wa Massage Parlor $227
Money tossed to bums $36.42
Father's Day gifts $0

TOTAL EXPENDITURE $111,177.42

1. TIME

A three hundred pound pro wrestler in lime green tights yanks the yarmulke off Jonathan Farb's head and with it a fistful of Jewfro. His name is The Big Samoan, and his legions of drunk fans cheer him on ringside: "Get that goddamn beanie! Jewboy's gotta learn!" Farb is fetal on the mat, his glasses shattered and hanging off his face, blood streaming from his nose and ears. The Samoan twirls the yarmulke on his fingertip, flings it casually into the crowd, then sweeps Farb's limp body up into the air to perform his signature Triple Suplex Of Death. The brain is made of soft, Jell-O-like tissue, but when Farb's head collides with the turnbuckle and the referee mercifully counts him out for "Three! Two! One!" grenade shrapnel explodes skullward.

Or at least that's how it felt.

Because when Jonathan Farb, a 34 year-old reality TV producer living in a pleasant home in the suburbs of Toronto woke to the sound of his five month-old baby wailing from his crib, the relentless stab of his migraine headache made him wish he was back in the ring. Farb peeled himself out of bed, popped a double ibuprofen and stumbled into Elliot's room. "Don't cry, baby. Daddy's coming, almost there." The baby, with his tufts of black hair, dark intense eyes and squeezable cheeks squirmed in a full diaper, but when his father arrived he squealed with delight. Even at his young age Elliot recognized comedy gold, and the mere sight of his clumsy dad fumbling his way through another diaper change filled him with joyful anticipation.

As for Farb, the agony of his migraine eased upon seeing his adorable son and then ebbed to a mild hum as he lifted the baby from the crib and up against his chest. Taking care of a kid was difficult for Farb—he always felt rushed and ineffectual, as if he were trying to thread a needle on a roller coaster. In other words, a pain in the ass. Even now he put Elliot's diaper on backwards and globbed on way too much diaper cream. But when Elliot was in his arms, the sweet butterscotch scent on top of his head and the way he so trustingly snuggled into the crook of Farb's neck gave him a sense of calm and clarity. He felt capable as a parent and masterful as a childcare provider—a kind of omnipotent deity—*whoa, do I smell diarrhea? My aching skull....*

To her credit, Farb's wife Shanna had laid out a full diaper bag for Farb's journey to the doctor's office. She left early for choir practice, ostensibly to work through her postpartum depression with songs of faith, but she had carefully organized hand-sanitizing gel, wet wipes, bottles, pacifiers, non-allergic formula, diapers, powder, Tylenol, an aspirator, thermometer, extra bottles, two changes of clothes and of course Elliot's beloved Cookie Monster, now more monstrous since Elliot tore off one of the eyes. There was even a note on the dresser with Elliot's vaccination record: *Dr. Arupal / 9 a.m. / North York General at Leslie and Sheppard / Fourth Floor / I'll be back sometime in the afternoon / Shanna.*

"Not an ideal father-son bonding excursion but I'll take it," Farb winced. Then, in a major act of independence, Farb laid Elliot down, changed the boy's outfit, re-diapered, clothed and fed him, all while kissing him a dozen times. The process (including a short drive to the hospital) took roughly two hours, and with the exception of only one near-death incident in which Farb discovered Elliot chewing on an electrical wire, things went off without a hitch. Who has never wanted to chew a bit of electrical wire?

"Elliot Farb?" The nurse called out, clipboard in hand. "Follow me." The room was bright aqua like the bottom of a pool and Farb recoiled at the florescent lights. His migraine picked up a sledgehammer and whacked at his frontal lobe. But with Elliot asleep in the portable car seat Farb forced himself to read over his pitch for only the twelfth time that morning. Nine years as a reality TV producer and Farb finally had a winner, a comedy competition show so TV-ready and so uniquely Canadian that even his ego-maniacal boss Larson agreed to let him pitch it to the Network. As Farb understood it there was only one obstacle to getting it green lit: *He needed to grow a pair.* The panic he felt, the way his voice quaked and his heart trembled every time he was asked to share an idea in front of a group had all but frozen a career that he suspected would blow up "if he only had a pair...." *Take that, Tin Man!* Larson knew of Farb's affliction and that's why he'd been able to hold Farb down for so long without a promotion to Executive Producer. If Farb wanted to thrive in TV, if he ever planned to get out from under Larson's massive thumb, he would have to stop hiding behind his tightly written proposals and finally speak up. Wednesday's Network pitch meeting was his big chance—if he failed he might as well settle into a life of dreary mediocrity and a ballessnes that would shut down Wimbledon.

§

When Elliot stirred Farb focused on the boy. Rocking Elliot softly, he leaned in and kissed his cheek with each forward motion. This boy. Farb knew he was genetically predisposed to obsess but Elliot was special wasn't he? What he respected most was how unapologetic he was. He laughed. He cried. He slept. He shat. He lived on intuition alone and was happy. Public speaking anxiety would be like a joke to him. But that's no surprise. The kid was clearly a fucking genius. Even now as Elliot woke from his nap Farb was sure his five-month old was thinking on a timeless conundrum that erudite men had spent decades pondering but had failed to solve. He certainly had solved the time-killing matter of having to look for a bathroom.

"Found a flaw in the theory of relativity?" Farb cooed. "Decoded infinity?"

But the answer soon came and it wasn't a gaffe in Einstein's theorem but a sickly sour smell that wafted into Farb's nostrils and worsened his grating headache. "Oh Jesus, again?"

Finally, Doctor Arupal, a wiry Indian woman sporting enormous Sally Jessy Raphael glasses entered the room looking down at her clipboard.

"Baby Elliot. Hmmm.... Hello, Daddy—nice to finally meet you. No Mommy today, eh?"

"She abandoned her child for choir practice," Farb smirked. "Hallelujah and all. Priorities, don't you know?"

"Oh, I can hardly blame her. With daddy off working until who knows when, it's good to have an extra-curricular activity. Good for baby too," Arupal jabbed. "So what have I heard about? Hives? Shouldn't be." The doctor checked Elliot's chart, then stripped him naked, weighed him, poked him, examined his ears and listened to his heart. "Looks good—gaining weight, strong, steady heartbeat. Seems like he's beaten this Failure To Thrive business."

"Good news."

"Proceed with caution though. The hives were likely a reaction to his latest medication so you should always check head-to-toe after anything new is ingested. We'll be moving to an antibiotic to settle this ear infection business, which should help him sleep better. Still, make sure to check his body often for reactions."

Farb nodded. He wasn't great at asking doctors questions but he did his best to think of something if only to induce Dr. Arupal into paying special attention to his son.

"What's his percentile in height and weight?" was all he could come up with.

"You want to hear he's going to be a six-foot-five genius?" Dr. Arupal smiled patiently. "The NBA, then a career in nuclear physics?"

"Wouldn't mind...."

Dr. Arupal ticked off boxes on a yellow sheet. "Let me see here. Height—sixty percentile. He's gaining weight at a good pace, fifty-five there. Good and average. He seems mature for his age, and observant. Should be smart. This is a boy who can probably do anything he wants in life."

"I knew it!" Farb let out a loud laugh and clasped his hands in joy.

"And how's Daddy's health?" Dr. Arupal said, still smiling, but it no longer extended to her eyes.

"Me? Great! My son's Michael Jordan, Superman and Abe Lincoln all rolled in one!"

"I saw your name in the computer. For an MRI? It says you keep rescheduling. Not wise."

"Well I don't," said Farb, "I never scheduled at all. I tried to get some migraine medication when Shanna was delivering and they haven't stopped calling me since. Those receptionists are like telemarketers—you ask for Aspirin and they want you to believe it's terminal."

"So what's the problem then?"

"No problem," Farb said, packing up. "Well, if Elliot's done we won't waste your time."

Dr. Arupal removed her enormous red glasses.

"It's just headaches," Farb sighed, pinching his temples. "If I spontaneously combust I'll take a cold shower, okay?"

"Lots of pain?"

"Some."

"Shooting pain or pressure? Stabbing? Show me where." At once the doctor moved from the baby to Farb, checking his ears, feeling around his temples and neck. "Yes, yes—I see you've been wincing from the lights. Does it hurt right here? How about here? Pressure?"

"You work with adults too?" Farb asked skeptically.

"I was head of neurology at the University of Mumbai. I come to Canada, well, they need baby doctors. A woman needs a paycheck so I am a baby doctor. Let's see here, how about your temples. Pain there mainly?"

"Yes, uh, I-I...."

The questions turned to more questions then a medical history survey then a visual exam then finally a neurological exam with a tomography X-ray. It was high-pressure sales. "How's this? Any pain here?"

"Yes, but I don't need...."

All in minutes Farb went from concerned parent to hyper-anxious patient, and holding Elliot close to his chest in the way that calmed him so much he was led from room to room deeper into the hospital's curtained antiseptic maze until he found himself lying alone on an MRI table wearing a heavy burgundy x-ray apron.

"What about the interminable waiting lists our socialized medical system is infamous for?" Farb said. "I guess it only applies to patients who *want* the treatment?"

"Try not to think about anything," Dr. Arupal spoke over an intercom. She was in a separate viewing room behind two inches of Plexiglas, rocking Elliot in her arms. Farb meanwhile lay in the exam room with a helmet-like contraption tightly enveloping his head on a movable table that guided him into a dark cylinder. The machine clanged and churned until Farb's head was set firmly in place. A claustrophobic's nightmare. Room 101.

"You finally got me!" he said, trying his best to stay calm. "How much are you going to charge the government for this? I feel my taxes skyrocketing as we speak!"

"Don't speak. It interrupts the waves. It will get quite loud."

"Where's Elliot?"

"The baby is fine," said Dr. Arupal. "Falling asleep."

"It's cold in here!" Farb said, trying not to panic.

"Please, no talking, Mr. Farb. We can bring you a blanket if you wish."

"Elliot?"

"Please no more words," said Dr. Arupal.

"Elliot!"

"He'll be fine. Now please be still Mr. Farb."

Farb sweated. The sweat leaked from his neck and poured rivulets down his back. The instinct to flee overcame him and his legs shook. How the hell had he gotten to this place? Wasn't he here for Elliot? The hives? Failure To Thrive? This was all a big mistake! He needed to get the hell out of here right now! And as the machine did its work on Farb's brain subjecting him to who knows what cancerous rays Farb saw only the terrible possibilities of his situation.

"ELLIOT? ELLIOT?" His body trembled. "ELLIOT!"

"Not yet, Mr. Farb."

Farb heard himself scream out but it was dull as if underwater, and when his knees and shoulders convulsed, smacking against the hard plastic cage it was a distant pain he felt. Farb experienced something akin to a fever dream–the sensation of being completely out of body and looking down on oneself. What he saw was a man who was not so young anymore–gray hairs creeping around his temples and a soft gut–well beyond the powers of a revitalizing steam bath or change in diet to perk him up. Worse, it was not the wizened look of a man who knew himself, who was bearing his age and scars with any grace.

"ELLLIOOOOOOOT!"

His body bucked against the MRI'S casket. Technicians ran this way and that to shut the machine down and extract him out of there before he injured himself. His mind was elsewhere, focused on the idea that he was being robbed. Life, as Farb understood it, was a massive jigsaw puzzle with one piece missing. That most of us never find out which piece is missing is a detail–there's enough frustration and hard work to make sense of the pieces you've got, but in the end locating that one piece is an obsession, a constant itch. Farb knew his itch well. He had attempted to assuage it by marrying Shanna, trying to treat her right, trying his best to commit to her, yet something was lost there. He had let too much slip, been too suspicious, punished her too often for his own insecurities. But Elliot. Farb understood that his missing puzzle piece could be found in giving himself wholly to this baby. To care for him more than even himself, to love selflessly, that was it. With Elliot's birth Farb's chance had finally arrived. But now God, that merciless misanthrope, had done it again, shortchanged him on his destiny and stolen away his missing puzzle piece. And as they lifted Farb's slack body from the MRI machine then revived him with cold dabs of water to his sallow forehead and finally smelling salts under his nostrils, Farb sprung awake like a Jack-in-the-box and there he saw it: through the fog and stars he came to focus on a distant object on the wall; it was more savage than regret, more callous than fear and pain; it hung pristinely gazing back at him like a hooded executioner. Tic Toc, Dad.

§

Farb gunned his Camry down the quiet tree-lined streets of York Mills towards Temple Beth-El. Elliot was in the backseat sucking a pacifier and sleeping off a long morning at the hospital, unaware of Farb's screeching turns or the revving engine as the suburban streets whipped by. Shanna's choir practice would still be in session for at least a half hour and Farb had to get there before it ended. The poor girl. She would be crushed! Nineteen when they met, Shanna barely knew how to take care of herself, let alone live without him–she would be so lost. Though it pained Farb to ponder, it passed through his mind that she might attempt suicide. "I'm her whole world!" Farb told himself. "What if she doesn't survive the news? Who will take care of the baby?" Farb wiped tears from his cheeks as he burned down Birchwood Road, mulling over all that happened only in the past few hours: sweating in the waiting room, rehydrating after his fainting spell, the hushed doctor's voices conferring over his results, new doctors called in, specialists scrutinizing MRI results, the waiting and finally Dr. Arupal sitting him down for the talk.

"I have some quite serious news," she said flatly, because she did not want to freak him out but didn't want to appear flippant either. "The MRI clearly shows a tumor in the right hemisphere of your brain. It appears to be contained, but I have to tell you that it is not small. Actually about the size of an acorn. It is pressing on sensitive areas, which is the cause of your headaches and perhaps other symptoms you may not be fully aware of. Undoubtedly you need a moment to digest all this?"

Farb sat there stunned and pale, tonsils swinging like a noose. Oh, Farb had time to "digest" it all right. Now would be a great time for his old college roommates to jump out and scream "Gotcha, Pussy!"

"At this point we don't know whether it's benign or malignant. If it is benign, likely a meningioma, it will not spread but it will grow, usually slowly, but sometimes more quickly. Nevertheless, it has to be treated or it can lead to permanent damage to your mental and physical functionality and eventually result in a pain-ful death. If it's malignant, the oncologist would almost certainly recommend surgery combined with chemo."

"I-I-I...."

"You may experience some delusions and erratic behavior in the future, which may make you unreliable to loved ones. This behavior might already have been occurring. Have you been extra moody lately? Emotionally mercurial?"

Farb, perhaps stunned by the use of the word mercurial, chose to ignore that little nugget. "How long do I have?" He felt like he was in a fucking soap opera. When the doctor's answer was "depends," Farb said, "If I go into a coma I want to be taken off life support. I want you to know that right now. I won't be a vegetable. I'm not going to learn to paint with my mouth or anything."

"Some say it's better than the alternative."

"Yeah? Well not for me." Then Farb got practical, his mind churning with possibilities. "My family is going to have to move to the States—cut into savings, put all of it into medical expenses for the best doctors...."

"Mr. Farb we have some of the best doctors in the world right here in Toronto."

"Heard that bit of propaganda before. I was waiting in an emergency room for six hours to have a piece of glass in my eye removed."

The Camry screeched into the parking lot at Temple Beth-El. Farb tried to pull himself together before he really broke down. He wanted to be strong for Shanna—assure her—tell her that he wasn't going anywhere. Tell her that it was all going to be okay. Only then could he attempt to convince himself of the same thing. Farb parked in a handicapped spot (fuck it, right?) and pulled the baby's car seat out, careful not to stir him. He marched up to the main synagogue entrance but found the big wooden doors locked. He went around the side. Two more entrance doors locked. He peered in the window—there seemed to be some movement but he couldn't make anything out. Around back he found a door wedged open with an orange pylon so he pushed it open with his shoulder and eased the baby seat in with him. The synagogue was empty save the distant sound of a vacuum cleaner. There were carpets all over the place so he just roamed. Farb liked Beth-El–the comfortable wall-to-wall carpeting gave it a relaxed feel so unlike the creaky cold wooden halls of the Conservative synagogue he'd been forced to attend as a child in Montreal. Five thousand years of Jewish suffering should suffice, time to walk around in socks, right? In the main sanctuary Farb found George, the janitor, vacuuming a single spot of carpet over and over again as if he was trying to catch a spider. George was Hispanic of some origin, was somewhat mentally challenged and always wore a shy boyish smile, a pressed short sleeve button-down shirt and a very visible Star of David on his neck chain. The congregants coped with George's awkward presence and his love of hanging people's coats at services, because they were in a house of God and worried that they would be judged, but also as a way to show the children that it's not nice to be unkind to anyone no matter how janitorial they looked.

Farb was no exception.

"Hey George. It's me, Jonathan Farb. Your, uh, friend."

George was startled by Farb's presence but smiled when he recognized him. "Mr. Farb! Mr. Farb! My friend!"

"That's right. Hey George, just looking for my wife. She's supposed to be in choir practice?"

"Uh, haven't seen Mrs. Farb this hour. No, not lately. Hmm.... Oh! Oh! Choir practice–that was cancelled a couple of hours ago– dental emergency, the Cantor had. Teeth falling out everywhere. Scary! They shut down rehearsal."

"I guess she's back at home napping. Thanks, George."

"No, she's at the dentist."

"Oh, I meant Mrs. Farb not the Cantor," Farb smiled. "Bye-bye George."

"I'm always here! Uh, Mr. Farb?" said George, concerned. "Can I hang your coat at the next Shabbat service?"

"You got it."

Back at the car Farb clipped Elliot's car seat in and was about to get behind the wheel when he winced at the recognition of yet another foul smell emanating from Elliot's diaper. "You've got to be shitting me." On cue Elliot began crying hysterically. "Okay, okay baby," Farb said in his hurried baby talk. "Just a quick diaper change, you know Daddy can do it." To make sure Elliot didn't squirm and get shit all over the car, Farb mixed a quick bottle with formula and popped it in Elliot's mouth. The screaming subsided as Elliot suckled, a pure relief.

Farb got to work. He lay Elliot on the back seat of the car, unbuttoned his Ramones onesie and removed the offending diaper. Suddenly the prospect of death didn't seem so bad. But as he was folding up the mess, Farb felt a cold wetness gush down over his hands. "Oh shit!" Somehow he hadn't screwed the top of the bottle on right and milk poured everywhere, all over Elliot's chest and onto his new clean outfit. Fucking nightmare. The child shrieked. "It's okay, it's okay." Farb plucked the seeping bottle from Elliot's hands causing his crying to intensify, then slid the diaper onto the floor as he fished for another outfit in the diaper bag. His hand slipped into the diaper, smearing yellowish poop on his fingernails and, when he flinched, onto the back of the driver's seat. He tried shifting Elliot's bum up so he could clean it with wet wipes while simultaneously pulling away his wet outfit and putting the new one on, but that caught the baby's arm in the seatbelt causing more panic. Farb's head pounded mercilessly. Then, through this whirlwind of shit and mess and screaming that arose out of nowhere, some odd intuition told him to look up from the baby through the backseat window.

In the distance, like a cavalry brigade rising on top of the hill, he saw Shanna.

She seemed to be coming up through the woods in the ravine behind the synagogue. She didn't appear rushed, just a little breathless–she stopped, looked down at her skirt and patted off some leaves. Even then, Farb admired her slim attractive figure, long swan-like neck and black curls that ran past her shoulders.

"Shanna!" Farb called out, hoping to hell that she would come over immediately and save him from this mess. But she was still far enough away that she couldn't hear him. "Shanna, I'm over here!"

It was her for sure. He could see that. Farb was about to pull the baby out of the car bare-assed and wave him over his head like a castaway firing his last flare when another familiar figured emerged behind Shanna. It was a man. Farb froze. "Shanna?" Before he even recognized the man there was something about the way they stood next to each other that alarmed him. Too close, too familiar. But even more he had a sickly gut reaction to the figure–short, heavily bearded with a tacky peach pastel golf shirt. Farb's heart pounced as he recognized Dr. Greenblatt, Shanna's obstetrician, the very man who delivered Elliot. Farb had privately nicknamed him "Toulouse Lautrec" for his diminutive size and rabbinical-length beard. Farb strained to make sure, but sure as those who Can-Can can Can-Can, it was him. He watched mesmerized as Greenblatt and Shanna talked for moment and then gazed in horror as Greenblatt put his arm around his wife's waist and kissed her on the neck. Shanna did not pull away–far from it–she giggled and pulled him in deeper. Then, quickly, the two jumped into a car and drove off.

For a minute Farb stood there transfixed, one hand half-changing Elliot's diaper, the other suspended motionless in the air. Had he just witnessed–? Did he just–? Did she just–? Did I happen upon the ultimate betrayal in marriage in broad daylight in the parking lot of my synagogue only hours after hearing a virtual death sentence from an Indian pediatrician? Farb's headache pounded like a fucking kettledrum. The baby yowled and it still amazed Farb how the sound of a crying baby can override everything no matter how profound. Farb crouched down and finished the job, chucking the dirty diaper on the pavement next to the handicap sign. He set Elliot back in the car seat with a bottle. "That conniving cunt!" he yelled. "I was her world!"

As Elliot settled into his bottle and new diaper, Farb got back in the driver's seat. He roared out of the parking lot, swung a left and drove east on the 401. He exited on Markham Road in the far reaches of Scarborough knowing that nobody would know him and he would know nobody. Old age homes receded into public housing, strip malls became check cashing and liquor stores. Farb was on the cusp of wall-punching rage so he wanted to be far from anyone he knew and this should be a safe zone. It was, after all, decision time and he needed perspective. He could turn the car around and race back home–he might beat Shanna there. Then what? A full-on confrontation? A full-on confession? If he got that on tape he could probably get custody of Elliot. But to what end? Revenge was a clear motive but Elliot would be the one to suffer if he ended up living with distant relatives or worse in a home. Plus it didn't escape Farb that if he went public with the affair he would be the object of pity and contempt at the office. There would be rumors of suicide if he didn't make it through his treatment, which would serve them right! John Gotti died of cancer in prison, maybe he could too as he served a sentence for offing a gynecologist who looked like a French painter?

There had to be a better way.

Farb flipped on his audio book *Advanced Hypnosis For Fear Of Public Speaking*. He wasn't supposed to listen to it while driving but he'd be damned if he was going to leave it at home or at the office where he would be exposed as a neurotic weakling. At first, the deep Australian voice soothed him: "You can look to the future where there is sooooo much more confidence for public speaking ahead, and I want you to count back from one hundred, letting each descending number relaaaaaaax you. One hundred, ninety-nine, ninety-eight...."

Farb took a left on Finch. The sky was getting gray and on the horizon black clouds gathered like parasites. Farb wanted to get out of the light, be in total darkness with dark people, do dark things. With Elliot in tow there would have to be a limit but he knew there were places men could go when they got like this—places that kept things safe.

The neon sign for Silver Spur Gentleman's Club featured a woman in a cowboy hat blowing a kiss: "Git Some!" Farb slowed the car. Elliot was calm and resting. He knew it was truly sick, definitely illegal, but if he put a blanket over the boy they might not even know. "Fuck it!" Farb took a deep hypnotic breath and pulled into the parking lot. "I'm dead anyway."

When Farb entered Silver Spur's carrying a car seat with a five-month old, even the Andrew Dice Clay-lookalike bouncer had to draw the line. "This had better be some kind of fucking joke," the bouncer said, stroking a knife scar along his jaw. Farb was about to tell him his best sob story about how in the last hour he had both caught his wife cheating and found out that he is going to die but instead he just pulled out his wallet. "Two hundred," he said. "I want to 'Git Some.'"

"There's a booth at the back. Baby starts crying and you're out on your ass."

Farb took a seat in a plush corner booth and while Elliot gazed off in fascination at the flashing red lights and the spinning disco ball above, onstage, "Tanya," in glass pumps and a pink boa gyrated to "Son Of A Preacher Man." Farb settled in with a twelve dollar beer and did what so many men do in need of perspective: stared at Tanya's vagina. It was an odd form of father-son bonding with Elliot, Farb knew, more than a decade premature, but he might not get an opportunity so distant in the future.

"So kiddo," he said, squeezing the baby's cheek. "You're probably wondering why I brought you here?" Elliot, who sucked happily on his pacifier, seemed to be listening. "What's that? No, no, Grandma isn't in the hospital. She's not even sick. Yes, yes, I know what I told your history teacher. Well, he lies too, albeit in a defeatist liberal way—I mean to deny the War of Civilizations. What was 9/11 for godsakes?!" Farb was off topic, but he'd never attempted to bond with his son on this level and politics seemed like a good place to start. Farb understood that to make it work, to really connect with the boy he would have to engage a part of his brain that he used mainly to come up with failed reality TV show ideas: his creative imagination. Baby Elliot had to be older, say a Senior in High School at very least. Farb had to imagine his teenage son into existence, make him real, delve into delusion, just as long as he was able to keep tabs on what was real and what was not. This might be his only shot. So he started over.

"Ah, that stuff isn't important. What matters, Elliot, is family, and what I am about to bestow upon you is part of your inheritance. It's why I paid the cover, bribed the bouncer and ponied up for a VIP booth. So sip your nine dollar Pepsi, try not to get bubbles on your fake moustache and experience a tradition as old as time. To some its lessons are responsible for the very survival of the species. My own father referred to it as 'The Birds and the Bees' but I've got a modern name for it colored by recent experience: How To Get Laid Without Getting Screwed!"

Farb liked the feeling of this. Pretending. He looked to his son and almost saw the fifteen year-old version of Elliot seated next to him. A tall, lanky basketball player–frayed baseball cap worn backwards, braces, light acne. It was all he had left.

"Now Son you've reached a certain age. Things have probably started to stir.... You've begun to notice girls, in particular that they have breasts and for whatever reason that this is a matter of great importance. You may feel the urge to reach out and give them a squeeze. Very natural. As you grow older these urges will become increasingly urgent until the immediacy upon which they must be satisfied will rule your very being: You will want them. You will want them now, you will want them well, and you will want them in great variety. None of this will change in old age. Your great-uncle Sid died begging his sixty-six year old night nurse for a BJ, but that's a story for another time. For now simply know this: the act of lovemaking can be a beautiful thing. Indeed there is nothing more intimate than two bodies thus entwined. It is a communication that transcends words, a sacred dance evoking the moon and stars, a gentle whisper from the God Eros that sends shivers into the flowerbed of the soul. And unless you get immensely lucky you will be doing it mostly alone."

Farb was starting to get looks from the bouncer. He bought a ten-dollar cranberry juice and tipped the waitress generously, who then nodded to the bouncer to get off his case. Farb winked at Elliot–the fifteen year-old next to him not the five month old strapped in a car seat. "My aim here is not to demystify the fairer sex for you, Elliot. Quantum physics would be more easily illuminated. What I offer is a simple roadmap so that you don't make the same mistakes I did. Understand that just as it is a natural part of men's genetic code to spread our seed as widely as possible, it is instinct for women to find a mate, procreate, and then nag relentlessly. When the French call an orgasm 'La petite mort' they are not referring to the orgasm itself but your life thereafter. Most men never propose marriage, they succumb. It was that way with your mother, FYI." Farb glanced up at the stage. "Take that redhead with the flaming anchor tattoo, the one picking up dollar bills manually? Looks like she's in for a good time? Don't kid yourself. She's one lucky lap dance away from a house in the suburbs, three kids and a Volvo. Find her a man willing to pay for it and she'll be remodeling the kitchen in no time, complaining about square footage. Women have power because while they may want sex, men need it. The mere suggestion of a naked body in bed drives men to madness–kingdoms fall for less than a thigh-flash and we're too horny to give a shit! Which brings me to my point: meet a nice Jewish girl, get married and provide me with a grandson as soon as possible. But in the meantime bed as many women as you'd like and bed them well. And if you happen to luck into a real live threesome grab onto it with a death-clutch and don't you ever let go. Because when that train leaves the station it's gone forever." Farb motioned again to the waitress. He was feeling good and could see from the way his son had turned his baseball cap around that he understood the lesson. "Two more please," Farb said. "And here's a little something for the redhead with the body art. Tell her 'nice job' from the two virile young gentlemen in the VIP booth."

Moments later the redhead arrived wearing little more than a sly smile. "You boys look like you've had a tough day, eh?"

"You don't know that half of it...."

But Farb wasn't done with his sentence before the redhead squealed with delight at the sight of Elliot. "Oh what a beautiful baby!" she cooed. "Those cheeks, so squeezable! He's got a *shana punim,* that's what my Jewish mother-law would say. And those eyes, hypnotic! He's what, six months?"

"Uh, almost...."

"Mine are already in high school if you can believe that. Both on the honor roll! My husband's always telling them 'you'll always be my babies,' but they're almost in university. He's a nut! Oh, but this one! Those cheeks!... Hey, Tiffany! Tanya! Get your bare asses over here, it's the Gerber baby!" In seconds Elliot was surrounded: "Oh, helloooooo my little boo-boo bubble boy, yes you're handsome! Soooo handsome, yes you are. Oh he's smiling at me! Tanya, he's smiling at me with that gorgeous *shana punim*!"

§

Farb emerged from The Silver Spur Gentleman's Club with a new sense of purpose in his short life. Sure, he might not be there until Elliot got old. He might not be able to throw around a baseball, attend his graduation at McGill or speak at his wedding. But he could take full advantage of the time he had. He swore there was some glimmer of recognition in the boy's eyes during their Birds and The Bees talk. He was convinced that if he just tried he could have some real impact before the illness took over. Maybe he could even outweigh some of Shanna's immoral influence since it would surely have its grip on Elliot when he was gone. "You can be your own man!" Farb told Elliot as he buckled him in. "Able to protect yourself against the Dark Side. At least that will be something. And what else do I have but you?" Farb's life may have been taken away, the sanctity of his marriage sullied, but Elliot was pure and innocent and was his to save. Farb pulled a pen from the glove compartment and scribbled down a list of the important issues he needed to cover by theme: Work, Health, Religion, Education, Manhood, Marriage, Money. He added an asterisk next to Money. Of all of the topics, that's the one that caused Farb's heart to panic. Yeah, he had life insurance but with a pending divorce Shanna would control that. He needed money that could be just for Elliot. To make certain that his child would be safe from the influences of the Dark Side. Independent from Shanna and Toulouse and his hypocritical oath. Real money. Fuck You Money. He needed to get it. For Elliot. And before it was too late. Farb grabbed his pitch document and clutched it to his chest. "Time to grow a pair, Farb," he said in the mirror. "Now or never."

Elliot was his to save. And it was time to go balls out. So Farb swung a left and headed down the Don Valley Parkway to the office with an urgency he hadn't felt in years. He flipped his audio book back on and contemplated his breathing from one hundred down to one.

2. TIME OFF

Shanna Farb woke up early that morning and slipped out of bed. Jonathan was twitching and moaning in his sleep as if he were in a death struggle with the devil himself, so she tiptoed out praying he wouldn't wake. Usually choir practice was held in the evenings, but this one morning the Cantor requested (as a special favor) that the choir convene early to work on some pieces for an upcoming recital. Of course Jonathan fought her on it—he had his super-important reality TV pitch to work on and blah, blah, blah.... Her first day off childcare in months and he had to bitch? His face made her want to puke. So Shanna snuck downstairs and packed a perfect diaper bag knowing that any excuse Jonathan would have to criticize her would be used as ammunition to strike back. It was a good plan. Shanna needed only to put distance between them while Farb tended to the incessant demands of a five month-old baby (and experienced briefly what she dealt with on a daily basis) and maybe he'd respect her for a minute and shut up.

But Shanna had another reason for leaving early, one that she hadn't even fully admitted to herself: the hope that she might run into Dr. Greenblatt again. It wasn't rational; she had no idea if he was the early type and she had only been to one rehearsal. She just hoped, that's all. At Shanna's first rehearsal, when she was introduced to the choir by the Cantor, she spotted him in the fourth row—that rabbinical-length beard, the pastel colored shirt, the general dorkiness—Dr. Raymond Greenblatt—the obstetrician who delivered Elliot to her. She was surprised to feel herself blush at seeing him again—maybe it was a reaction to the sour memory of the hospital, the difficulty of breastfeeding, the intimacy of what he'd seen of her marriage, not to mention her anatomy.

It all came rushing back. But, beyond that, Shanna recognized the excitement.

"Let's welcome the newcomer," the Cantor had said. "Shanna, if you can find a place in the second row? Maybe you can just listen for a while then feel free to join in whenever."

Shanna stepped nervously into line, grabbed a blue music binder and flipped to the Hebrew. The choir began to sing "Shalom Aleichem." A familiar song from her Reform upbringing in Montreal. She listened at first to the others, gauged her place in the harmony and, after only a few lines, entered with her sweet high voice. It all felt very natural, like she'd been missing the whole time. But as she sang, Shanna could feel Greenblatt stealing glimpses of her, a warm sensation at the back of her neck. She looked up from her binder, turned back towards him and caught him smiling, shaking his head in a kind of sweet disbelief.

"Mimelech mal'achei ham'lachim / Hakadosh baruch Hu...."

Today, at her second practice, it was no different. When Shanna arrived at the synagogue, surprised to see that everyone was already in place (the walk had taken longer than planned), she saw him there in the fourth row smiling as sweetly as before, nodding to her as she made her way to her place in the choir. "Just getting started," intoned the Cantor. This time Shanna found herself even more conscious—but also more aroused by Greenblatt's stares. She found herself trying to look more attractive as she sang her part in the harmony—sucking in her cheeks, pushing out her chest. She glanced his way as she flipped the pages in her blue binder and couldn't help but smile as she met his eyes. It was so electrifying that Shanna sang with a surprising strength and assurance. The mournful Kaddish seemed more powerful than ever.

When Greenblatt approached her at break Shanna was so flustered she spilled her coffee.

"If I didn't see you with my own eyes I wouldn't believe it," Greenblatt smiled. "I'm thinking to myself that can't be Shanna Farb? She just delivered and she looks like an aerobics instructor."

"Post-Natal Pilates. You'd be surprised," Shanna laughed, thankful she'd found a quick retort, but then adding oddly, "And my maiden name is actually Mandelbaum."

"Oh, well good to know!" Greenblatt smiled as if this added info was a gift. "You look amazing."

"You said that already."

"Oh."

"But continue if you must!" Shanna joked, playful now. "I think there's a dart board with my picture on it in the maternity ward at Toronto General."

"Still the comedian!" Greenblatt laughed. "And your singing voice! You must be a professional?"

"You should see me dance. I'm thinking of taking my act on the road. Got a van?"

Greenblatt burst out laughing again, and Shanna chuckled nervously as she looked around the break room—they were making a bit of a scene, but it still seemed friendly, not out of bounds for two married people.

"You have a very nerdy laugh," she pointed out.

"Yes, I'm afraid so."

Shanna looked the doctor up and down—old but not too bad. *With a little grooming....* Guilt cut off the thought so she forced out a question she didn't care to have answered. "Have you been in choir a while?"

"Three years," Greenblatt replied. "My wife Carol got me into it. She was the songbird. Wouldn't miss a practice. Then one morning she just woke up and said, 'You know, I'm done with the choir.' Moved onto something else. Painting. Has a whole studio set up in the garage. Very talented–abstract stuff. I'm not like that, not able to just stop something out of nowhere and move on. Takes me longer to get comfortable and then I get so attached. Plus painting, I don't know it's so, so...."

"Lonely," Shanna said.

"Right. Lonely. I need to be with people."

Their eyes met a fraction of a second too long and now Shanna blushed. "We'd better get back."

But just as Shanna said that some commotion broke out in the break room. Several choir members were down on their hands and knees searching the carpet for a crown that had fallen out of the Cantor's mouth while biting into stale ruggelach. "You might have swallowed it," one of the congregants suggested. "This same thing happened to my cousin Shelly. I know a brilliant periodontist–Jewish and single if you know anybody for him?" The Cantor, who was in obvious pain, complaining that her tooth felt cold and exposed, shuffled out to the hall, embarrassed, then emerged several minutes later to announce that she had scheduled an emergency dental appointment ("Thank *Hashem*!"), and would have to reconvene practice on Tuesday night, she was sorry for the inconvenience.

"Well," said Greenblatt, chuckling a bit. "What do we do now?"

There were some rumblings to keep the practice going without the Cantor but that dissipated as everyone seemed to have somewhere to go anyway, something to do, something pressing. Everyone but Shanna. "Gorgeous day for a walk?"

§

The ravine was crisp and wet, matted with yellow leaves. Squirrels scurried up the maples and there was the smell of a distant campfire. Shanna and Greenblatt walked silently along a trail that was used by the local Equestrian Center. They kept focus on the ground, swerving to avoid the frequent plops of horse dung. "Yeah, really gorgeous out here this time of year," Greenblatt joked, sidestepping a still-steaming pile.

Shanna kept her head down and nodded. She was aware that this was an illicit walk, that she was concerned someone might see them and then what would she say? He's my friend, he's my friend. Couldn't she at least pretend to be the old Shanna from her younger, happier days–who had a tongue ring and gallery representation as an edgy up-and-coming visual artist with a knack for one-liners? For one solitary moment was she not permitted to share time with a man who seemed genuinely interested in what she had to say and laughed at her jokes and not be Mrs. Farb, suburban mom held captive by a husband who lives to pitch reality TV shows? Even now as she took a lovely nature walk completely free of her husband, she felt the weight of him, a smug grin that told her that the very silence of her walk with Greenblatt, the sound of every squish of mud or crack of tree branch underfoot was a confirmation of how dull and self-centered she was. "Give it up–you're not that fun anymore." She blamed it all on Jonathan–he'd been hammering at her confidence for years. Fuck him! Shanna would be damned if she was going to let this chance at adult companionship slip her by. She forced a smile and just began talking.

"I had a ravine just like this behind my high school," she said. "It was my rebellious teenage getaway with my girlfriends. We would all put on slutty clothes and makeup, climb down after school and smoke cigarettes. Big rebellion! I remember the last time we went down there one of the girls stole a joint from her parents. So we all started smoking it and one of the teachers, a younger guy with sideburns, came down the path."

"Uh-oh!"

"That's what we said! Of course we were mortified–we'd be expelled, jeopardize our educations and our parents would kill us. Instead, the teacher just asked for a puff. We thought it was a trap of course, but he just took the joint and talked about summer vacation as if nothing was happening at all. Anyway, years later he married one of the girls in that ravine, Cindy Resnick. And it was this huge scandal, but not because he had been her teacher at all–he just wasn't Jewish. Her parent's wouldn't hear of it so the poor guy had to convert and got circumcised at like thirty years old! Apparently they buried the foreskin under a tree in that ravine. Bizarre."

Greenblatt burst out laughing. "That's the craziest story! You missed your calling."

Shanna laughed too. "Yeah, you know why? Because I just made the whole thing up."

"What? Why?!"

"No clue. Something about this situation makes me want to show off."

"I should have known," Greenblatt laughed. "The thought of you smoking weed–total joke!"

"Why? I don't seem badass enough? I smoked opium in Malaysia with hill tribesmen when I was nineteen. But now? Read the headlines: 'Suburban house mom arrested for smoking drugs.' They'd throw away the key!"

"Not if we don't get caught," Greenblatt said.

"Ha! You're fucking with me."

"I have a friend in anesthesiology. He has access to all this high-grade medicinal stuff, very mellow. I use it to relax once in a while. And it does make choir practice so much more enjoyable." Greenblatt reached into his pocket and pulled out an Altoids tin with three rolled joints. "Wanna party?"

"You've got to be fucking with me."

§

Shanna and Greenblatt sat on a damp log surrounded by bright yellow leaves and blew gales of smoke into the autumn air.

"Jonathan hates you, you know," Shanna reflected, passing off the joint. "He felt like you were fighting him in the hospital. He was obsessed with it. Actually, I thought it was kind of typical and hilarious. Two macho men going toe-to-toe in a delivery room."

"I may have been trying to show off a bit too. You kind of bring that out in me," Greenblatt admitted.

"Well, whatever it was, you got to him. I mean he was so pissed!"

"He tried to bribe me, you know? Wanted to change your son's medical record, which isn't even my department. He wanted it to say that the baby had chronic diarrhea instead of Failure To Thrive. Why, I have no clue. Didn't like the sound of it? He offered me Raptors tickets!"

"Oh, that is so Jonathan!" Shanna laughed, then got serious. "What did you think of us, Ray? I mean you've probably seen hundreds of young couples having a baby. You must have an opinion of us in particular. How did we act in there?"

"It was pretty plain to me," said Greenblatt, his voice raising an octave as he exhaled a plume of smoke. "I think that with couples, often, there's one who isn't totally valued. In your case, you are bursting with life, so funny and disarming and kind and your partner doesn't really value that except if it reflects well on him."

"Jonathan? He used to, you know? He supported my art when we were in Montreal—used to drive me to far-off galleries and come see my performances. Even the one where I was dressed up like a porpoise to sing "Les Miz." Now he's always suggesting I join these Mommy & Me groups or learn to knit like I'm going to be sitting there doing nothing but thinking about him and Elliot. Ha! Imagine me knitting? And besides with all the laundry, the cooking, paying bills, doctor's visits, there's never a single minute to just—"

"Focus on yourself?"

Shanna chuckled. "Now I'm a cliché! Like every whiney middle class mom with too much time on her hands."

"You have no idea how unique you are," Greenblatt said. "So it's a shame that your husband objectifies you. But of course that's classic for a narcissist."

"How did you catch that so quickly? It's like you're so insightful.... *Whoa, I'm high!*"

"Not charming. As to the first, it's transparent. And for the second, you are unique. Strong, funny, intelligent, astonishingly beautiful. You just have too much on your plate. And you need a break."

"Wait, wait—did you just call me astonishingly beautiful?"

Shanna burst out laughing, remembering in a flash that it was a similar line Jonathan fed her when they met eons before, and Shanna wondered if she lived by a script and if she did... was she falling for her obstetrician? Yellow leaves twirled from the sky onto Shanna's sweater. She caught one in her hand—wide and cold and wet and pure. It tingled her on her fingertips. Greenblatt leaned over to touch the leaf, too, and instead took her hand.

"What are you doing?" Shanna said.

"I guess I'm trying to make out with you."

Shanna let out a great snorting drugged-out laugh. "Make out?! Is this 1957? You want to go steady after that? I'm married. I have a baby. How old are you anyway?"

"I guess too old." Greenblatt pulled his hand away, hurt.

"Oh, you wounded puppy! What about your wife? Would she be okay if you just made out with some member of the choir?"

"Carol? Oh, our relationship ended years ago. We just stay together for the kids. Now that they're off at school she's pretty much lost interest in me completely. Moved on."

"Like she did with singing in the choir?"

Greenblatt shrugged, acknowledging the connection.

"This is so fucked up," Shanna said, and watched Greenblatt's face light up like a child's as she leaned in to kiss him. It was wrong; indeed fucked up. But why not? She could be with Farb forever and never get a moment like this. Never be wanted like this. Greenblatt was so admiring, so attentive with her. Jonathan only made her feel small.

They kissed passionately and clumsily like high school kids. Greenblatt moaned as he felt Shanna's breasts. And with the wild haze of high-grade medicinal marijuana loosening their inhibitions Shanna and Greenblatt fell to their knees and rolled around in yellow leaves like they were in the coat check at a smoke-filled loft party in Montreal's Mile End and life had no consequences.

3. WORK

Elliot lay on the carpet of Farb's office ogling a stack of DVDs that represented much of Farb's resume in reality TV: *Hockey Star Rumble, Canadian Idol, Project Runway (Canada)*, and who could forget three seasons on *Pamela Anderson: Canadian Daughter*. Farb splayed out dozens of DVD cuts and finally understood the reason he'd kept them so long: childcare. As light refracted in dizzying rainbows off the silver discs, the baby cooed and giggled, genuinely pleased. This freed Farb up to rehearse his big reality pitch for the thirty-ninth time: "Canadians are a multi-talented people. But one of our nation's greatest gifts is something that we often apologize for. Canadians are masters at the art of Apology and it's time we learn to brag about it."

The concept for "Canada's Next Great Apologist" was comedy first and foremost. Something Farb dreamed up in the shower and just didn't stop being funny to him. But then it started to make sense. American's are always making fun of their shortcomings (*Are You Smarter Than a 5th Grader?* comes to mind), so why not Canadians? Farb drafted up a basic format–twelve contestants all vying to win the Grand Prize of a high paying job as Canada's Chief Apologist. The contestants would compete in making apologies not only to people in their lives but to entire populations, like the First Nations, or the ancestors of the Chinese immigrants who worked on the Trans Canadian Railroad. A celebrity panel would judge each contestant's tact, their emotional sincerity and ability to derive an acceptance from the people to whom they apologized. At the end of each episode one contestant would be eliminated and apologized to profusely until they had a winner.

Farb knew the pitch had a real chance to be green lit. The human story was there, the Canadian angle was a lock–he even had ideas for talent. He knew that CANT (The Canadian Association Of Network Television) was searching desperately for Canadian-content that would boost ratings and that, thanks to CANT's longstanding relationship with Gordon TV Productions (Gordon was a CANT hero back in the '80s), they were sure to pick up at least one show idea before the end of the quarter. If the Apologist was green lit and had only a few seasons, as Creator, Farb would get some nice residual checks and be able to afford Elliot a good start in life. The boy would be able to make his own decisions in life and Shanna and Toulouse would be powerless to control him.

Only nerves stood in Farb's way. When Larson handed him the floor in front of the Network Execs on Monday just which Farb would show up? Sharp, creative Farb with a great idea in his pocket? Or bumbling sweaty Farb incapable of breathing and dead in the water when it came to presenting an idea with confidence? Every public speaking book said that practice is the most important way to overcome performance anxiety. So Farb repeated his pitch over and over, committing it to memory so that when his big moment came he would be on auto-pilot: "Canadians are a multi-talented people. But one of our nation's greatest gifts is something that we often apologize for."

Farb edited the wordy bits, smoothing over rough transitions and committing them to memory. When Elliot whined, Farb rocked him in his arms or changed him or made him a bottle. The new antibiotics that Dr. Arupal had prescribed for Elliot's ear infection seemed to be working wonders–Elliot's naps were stretching to several hours and he seemed relatively comfortable when he was awake. Farb should really get the boy a crib if he was going to bring him to the office regularly. Something with a music box.

Farb worked feverishly. He worked until the baby slept, woke back up and slept again. He worked over pots of sour coffee and stale cookies. He worked even as his migraine almost blinded him and the pills failed to soothe his head. Around ten p.m. Farb noticed his cell phone light up.

It was Shanna.

For a moment Farb just held the phone to his chest. He wasn't sure how he was going to deal with hearing her voice after what he saw, but it would be suspicious not to answer. Surprisingly, when Farb did pick up his voice was measured and calm, it was Shanna who was frantic. "Where the hell are you?" she said. "I've called all day! It's after ten! Is Elliot okay? I phoned the hospital and they told me to call you but you were nowhere. What's going on? Why aren't you home? Why did the hospital say to call you? Why didn't you pick up? I've tried to reach you over and over!"

For a moment Farb imagined that Shanna was sneakier than he gave her credit for–to act frantic, accusatory, that was a good tactic for someone who had just banged an OB/GYN. But looking at his phone he noticed that there were eighteen missed calls and a dozen messages and he hadn't called home once.

"Everything's just fine," Farb peered over his desk and saw that he'd left a milk bottle stuck in Elliot's mouth. He tiptoed over and removed the choking hazard. "I'm at the office with Elliot just catching up on some work. The doctor said the hives were just a reaction to that old medication. She gave me a new antibiotic and he seems to have mellowed considerably–or maybe it's just the company."

"Why did the hospital ask me to call you, Jonathan?"

Hmmm, somehow Farb hadn't thought through what *his* alibi would be. He certainly didn't want to tell Shanna about his prognosis–that would be far too generous. He wanted her to know last, maybe from a stranger, maybe from the coroner. He wanted her to suffer humiliation and guilt for betraying him and what's more for fucking the baby doctor.

"This is not easy for me to say," Farb said, "But we're going to have to find a new pediatrician."

"Doctor Arupal? Why?"

"She's smug and patronizing that's why, and we got in a fight."

"She's been Elliot's pediatrician since the beginning. She's wonderful to him. What happened?"

"Look, I don't have a hell of a lot of time to talk about this but we got in this huge blow-up about sleeping habits and I just didn't like her attitude. She told me maybe I should see another doctor if that's the way I feel. I'm already getting references for doctors closer by."

"I don't know what to say."

"Just don't call her office anymore. There might be issues transferring Elliot's medical records if I piss her off again and I don't want you to complicate things."

There was a pause in the conversation in which both Farb and Shanna were at a loss for words. After the initial hysteria of getting a call from the hospital, Shanna hadn't had time to think about how she was acting, whether or not she was revealing anything to Farb or betraying that her lips still felt raw from Greenblatt's beard, not to mention that she was still coming off a buzz from the joint she'd smoked. "When are you coming home?" she said finally.

"Don't wait up. Elliot's sleeping well. I've got a makeshift crib set up for him. I might just stay put for a while."

"Okay. Well, let me know."

Farb hung up. He tried to focus again, get back to his pitch but, instead, he walked over to where Elliot slept on the floor and sat there next to him. Sure he could ruminate about Shanna's call, get angry and jealous and plot revenge, but there were more important things to do. He had a son to raise.

"Even if this show gets picked up," he said to Elliot, who snored steadily. "Even if there's a good sum of cash for you in the future, you're going to have to make your own money. You know that, right? None of this trust fund kid crap. You're going to have to go out there and work for yourself. Learn the value of money. I know how things go. You'll go off to college and all those crazy left-wing professors will get you all turned around. You'll say you don't want to work for The Man, that you want to 'live simply so that others may simply live.' But if there's one thing I know for sure, Elliot, it's that you will work for The Man someday. It just depends *which* Man you'll work for and in what capacity—as a complete loser in the belly of the beast, or as a player with some control over your destiny and a stash of hotties blowing up your cell."

Farb took a deep breath. He felt another father-son talk taking form: Education. But with Elliot fast asleep he decided not to depend on osmosis for this one. So he picked up a pen and wrote Elliot his first letter:

Dear Son,

You may not find this letter until after you have already moved into your dorm. The daze of class registration and freshman orientation is likely upon you, not to mention a flurry of Frosh Week trim. There's a reason I hid this letter in a box of Trojans—it's likely the first place you'd check. But this letter exists not to keep tabs on your sexual adventures (how could anyone fully keep track?), but to offer guidance and a swift kick in the ass as you sally forth into your first year of university: Son, you made it into McGill. I'm proud of you—now don't screw it up.

You will learn much over the next four years, Elliot. There is no limit to what you may absorb if you commit to expanding your intellectual horizons. Dig deep into the works of The Greats. Plato. Hawkings. Descartes. Of course it's up to you to decide which of these great thinkers are seekers of the truth and which are masters of bullshit. For the most part, the world of academia is a strange and disorienting place: an anti-meritocracy where frustrated failures too incompetent to make it in the private sector hold court. Their shaggy beards and corduroy blazers emblems of inadequacy, they distort facts in a way that justifies their miserable beings—if the capitalist system is flawed then that explains why they never got their book published or became the millionaire they secretly aspired to be. They are smug and delusional and, worse, they are tenured! Ignore most of what they tell you. But study hard. You will need good grades to land a high paying job. And even if at times it all seems like a bizarre exercise in counter-intuitive memorization where one plus one equals three, remember that the answer is, and will remain, two, that they are completely fucked in the head but that business is business.

And soak up the knowledge! To be erudite is a lofty goal, a tradition of your ancestry. Jews are known as "The People of the Book" for a reason and so long as there is a nubile blonde out there willing to trade a titty-flash for good study notes we will remain thus. Many a Bloomfeld and Lipschitz (and Farb!) *have gotten laid for no other reason than they gave good math tutorial. Look at Einstein. Marilyn Monroe famously called him the sexiest man alive. Then she married Arthur Miller, another Yid. And remember Elliot that you have a responsibility to represent the Farb name. I don't need to remind you that you are fourth generation McGill dating back to your great-uncle Milt Farb who studied to be an engineer in 1922. In the U.S., your Legacy Status would increase your chances of acceptance big time, but in Canada, backward socialist nation that it is, your legacy is perceived as privilege, which takes a hard backseat to racial quotas. If you were a green Cyclops of indeterminate gender and a gimp leg, you'd be on full academic scholarship I assure you. How ironic it is that when your grandfather Abe applied to McGill in 1933 only three Jews were allowed in Dentistry. Did he complain? Are there* reparations for him? *No*. He competed for one of three spots and got it. Jews are a racial minority only when it counts against us. We are discriminated against for being a minority and then we are discriminated against because we aren't considered a minority! It's an alarming double standard but don't kid yourself into thinking anyone gives a shit, not even your liberal co-religionists.

Finally, keep your grades up. You can count on the same system of financial reward that we agreed upon in high school ($50 for B+, $75 for A-, $200 for an A). In fact you can up it by a C-Note, but it works the other way for poor grades so keep a buffer in your savings account for checks headed my way too. Which reminds me—the enclosed Gold Card is for school-related purchases ONLY. I don't mind a meal now and then, you may buy more rubbers at the local drugstore but as for regular offerings to the God Bacchanalia you will budget that into the generous monthly nut that I am already transferring to your Royal Bank account.

Devour this experience Elliot—let the world's riches unfold before you in a great wave of scholarliness and spiritual cultivation. Oh, and if reading this letter in any way delayed you from deflowering some hot sorority chickadee—resume with vigor!

Carpe Tuchus!
Your Proud Father

4. CAROL

Dr. Raymond Greenblatt sat in his basement office absolutely buzzing. He'd smoked another joint on the ride home from Temple Beth-El just to savor the perfection of his dalliance with Shanna Farb and it heightened the sensations considerably. The guy couldn't believe his luck! Not since his first years at Toronto General when a few nurses singled him out as the new young doc on the block did he receive attention from anyone approaching Shanna's beauty. And now finally, after years of staying relatively thin, jogging the treadmill three times a week and drinking revitalizing tonics, he was getting what he deserved: a hot young piece of ass to have sex with! Greenblatt wasn't delusional. He knew the marijuana was key to the seduction. Hell, he wasn't sure he would have landed Carol without his little green helper and he was glad he had the foresight to bring some pinners to choir practice just in case. But, dammit, maybe he didn't even need the weed! Maybe, just maybe, Shanna Farb, that Goddess with long black curly hair, tight high ass and soft swan-like neck would want him even without the thigh-loosening haze of drugs! His father always told him that a man's value increases with age and it was as true now as it was when he said it years ago. But Greenblatt just had to know: had he really become, at fifty-one, a swordsman? Perhaps Shanna was only the beginning of his triumphs! The younger nurses at the hospital had been giving him new looks lately, complimenting him on his beard, laughing a little bit longer at his stale puns! He might have them all! An orgy of supple young flesh! But let's not get ahead of ourselves. First job was to make sure Shanna Farb was a sure thing. To have her waiting in his bed, on his arm at hospital fundraisers, hell, back to his high school reunion so that he could watch the

Prom King with his bum knee and hag wife just burn with jealousy. That would be the best!

Greenblatt opened his desk drawer and removed a velvet case containing one of the War II-era pistols he spent much of his free time collecting. He polished it with a felt cloth and expensive cream he bought on special order. When he found an antique store on Queen Street West that specialized in just this kind of thing, it was too intriguing to pass up. Even as he doubted the guns' authenticity he happily coughed up the cash because when he fondled them he felt like a tough Jew, like if he was back there in Poland, he would discard his spectacles, grab a gun and kill those fucking Nazi bastards. It was why he grew his beard so long: as a wink to the Radical Jewish Underground of badass muthershtuppers!

Yes. This was Greenblatt's favorite time—when he could hide in the quiet refuge of his unfurnished basement with its naked pavement floors, exposed wall wiring and rusty artifacts and polish his pistols. Today it was his Karabiner-S43 that he slowly stroked. The elderly arthritic man who found him the piece went so far as to claim that the man who'd owned it had held Goebbels in the crosshairs of his rifle in a small village in Uruguay, but had been called off by Israeli Intelligence at the last second. Greenblatt doused a special extra-strength lubricant on the pistol and could almost imagine himself shooting Goebbels himself. Maybe Shanna could sense in him the brave hero who would surely pick a up a gun to defend her too? Sure that arrogant asshole Jonathan Farb might be younger than him and may have taken a karate lesson or two, but when it came to cold hard violence, caveman shit—Greenblatt was the Alpha. He raised his pistol to the naked overhead bulb, pinched an eye closed and imagined finding Shanna held up by a gang of murderous thugs in an alley and *POW! POW! POW!* gunning them down one by one. "My hero!" Shanna would say between kisses.

"My big Jewish bearded hero! Take me right here, now—let me fellate you in this grimy alley! It's for both of us!" Greenblatt felt a boner coming on and even considered using some of his pistol lubricant on himself to consummate the fantasy when a loud *THUD* sounded from upstairs that broke his concentration. "What the hell?" Greenblatt's mood darkened immediately. He packed away his pistol and climbed the creaky stairs so miffed that, frankly, it messed with his high.

What he found as he entered the hall was his wife Carol cleaning the storage closet so furiously it made Greenblatt freeze in his steps. "What the...?" Jackets were hurled to the floor in big piles, boxes with boots turned over and shaken violently, bags beaten to a pulp of compliance until they were just sheets of fabric and leather. Grunts and snorts emanated from inside the closet as Carol hefted old suitcases that had been there for decades and then stuffed them inside bigger suitcases to make more room. "I'm cleaning out your closet!" Carol huffed, not even bothering to turn around to greet her husband. "What a mess! It's been bothering me for years. Did you even know that we had this much luggage? I'm going to take your winter jackets to the dry cleaner—they're filthy. That will be the third time I've been to the cleaners this week. At fourteen dollars a jacket that's what, two hundred dollars with shirts and pants? Adds up. I think we have moths, so maybe I should just throw the whole lot out—what a waste. This makes me so sick. I could die thinking about the waste!"

Awed by the sheer intensity of her movements, Greenblatt stood back and gazed at his wife of more than twenty years. Could he be married to her? She looked like his grandmother: color drained from her skin, her hair straw copper, her ass a jiggly shapeless rump in gym shorts and old ratty sneakers. What grossed-out Greenblatt the most was her skin color—it was if she'd been flushed of her natural pinkness and had it replaced with a yellow and orange blotchiness. None of that affected her energy level however, which was dizzying. As Carol ripped apart an enormous cardboard box with thick manly hands, Greenblatt thought he heard her slip a fart. What did it matter? There was no shame left in his marriage, no romance or hope that things would improve. Carol left out her menopause medication for chrissakes. There was a time before her looks became irreversible that she did talk about getting some plastic surgery—her nose had dropped a good quarter-inch over the years adding a small dollop of flesh hanging over her upper lip and Greenblatt hoped that she would opt for more surgery once she went under, like a boob job or liposuction. But just as soon as she'd brought it up she changed her mind about the whole thing. "Oh, I'll just age gracefully," she said with a glint of pride in her eyes that sickened Greenblatt. "It's not like I have anyone to impress!"

As for their sex life, Greenblatt did his best to keep up the loose twice-monthly schedule they'd kept for years, but more and more he felt that it was a drag. Instead of expending the energy to mount her as he had who knew how many hundred times, lately, he just hinted at blowjobs, which Carol surprisingly acquiesced to, though with little flare.

"A little help wouldn't hurt?" Carol said, poking her head out of the closet.

"Huh?" Greenblatt tried to snap out of his dark thoughts. "Oh, of course. Sorry." He got down on his hands and knees and began folding bags for storage that he didn't want or feel he'd need in his lifetime.

"Just stack 'em up and I'll do the rest," Carol instructed. "Oh Raymond! I haven't eaten, not a thing. Mario from the gym told me to eat when I'm being very active like this but I feel good doing it. Like I work better on less food. Do I look thinner? Oh, but I better have a nibble before I go to the bank, then the post office, then to return those shoes. Did you even notice that the fridge is empty again? I guess you never picked up the cottage cheese like I asked you to?"

Greenblatt had no memory of it.

"Great. Well, that's another stop I'll have to make. Your mother insists on organic cottage cheese when she visits and then barely eats it. You'll carry the grocery bags in from the driveway. Oh I'm so glad I'm finally doing this. If I didn't clean it myself then it would just sit there for eternity, stewing. Imagine the mold!"

"We have mold?"

"You know what I mean!"

Greenblatt willed himself to descend further into the small buzz he'd created from his second joint to avoid Carol's hyper-intensity but instead he made the tragic mistake of persuasion by rational analysis. "But Sweetie, we never even use this closet. Don't you think it's a bit irrational to let it bother you so much?"

Carol looked at her husband stunned like he'd asked what in the world we need air for? "Raymond," she sighed. "If I feel like the closet needs cleaning, then it needs to be cleaned. Those are my feelings. Feelings are never wrong. Not ever. Isn't that what the therapist helped you see in our last session?"

"She said that feelings are always real but not always rational."

"Is that how you interpreted it? Figures. You weren't even listening. At a hundred-twenty dollars a session! Because I spoke to her on the phone for an hour after the session and she thinks you have major problems to work out that start with your parents' divorce."

Greenblatt dodged that old trap. Every time he showed the slightest rebellion against her, Carol wanted to drudge up the particulars of his parents' divorce over forty years ago. How about this?: They hated each other. They got a divorce. They hated each other less. End of story.

Greenblatt was about to question Carol's personal relationship with their marriage counselor when Carol suddenly stopped her work and began sniffing the air around her, "Why were you in the ravine?" she asked.

Greenblatt's heart vaulted. "Uh... not exactly sure what, uh, you mean?"

"I smell horse manure Raymond. You know how hypersensitive my nose is. And there's only one place around with horses nearby and that's the ravine behind the synagogue. I hope you didn't drag any into the house. I just had the carpets cleaned. And look at the stain on your pants. Did you fall?"

Greenblatt looked down at his pants–grass and mud smudges displayed prominently on his knees–there was even a yellow leaf stuck in the pleat of his pants. He hadn't noticed. "Oh!" Greenblatt said, his voice aflutter. "Can you believe... we were locked out of the synagogue? Yeah, uh, the front door is broken and the janitor was supposed to be there. So I-I-I... had to open a basement window just to get us in for choir practice. Got right down on my knees in the leaves and mud!"

"You're lying to me Raymond," Carol said, bored.

"No, no I'm not."

"Your voice is nervous and it just sounds too peculiar."

"Well life is peculiar Carol," Greenblatt said, then couldn't believe his stupidity. His next move was to attempt an escape but Carol stopped him again.

"You know, I'd like to join again I think," she said.

"Eh?"

"The choir. Yeah, I think it would be fun. Plus it would be a lovely way to spend more time together. Isn't that what the therapist encouraged us to do? Spend more time doing something we both enjoy?"

"But what about your painting? You're doing so well."

"That can wait Raymond. Our relationship is much more important."

"Well if you really want to maybe you can join after Sukkot? We've already learned so many new songs–you'll find it hard to catch up."

"I can hold my own. I'll learn the songs from your blue binder. Besides, it's what I want so I'm going to do it."

"Of course," Greenblatt said. Then he turned to leave.

"Oh, Raymond? When you get the cottage cheese can you also go to Shopper's Drugmart and pick up my prescription? It's right next door."

"Of course, Dear."

§

Greenblatt paced the backyard. He needed some air or, most likely, to get high again. Is it possible she already knew? Did Carol have that much control over his mind? Was it already over? It was just like her to take away his one joy before it even really blossomed, to ruin his life (again!) and weigh him down with her misery. Greenblatt looked up at the sky maybe to pray and he noticed dark clouds looming. That had to be a sign. Or maybe just divine instruction to move his rendezvous with Shanna indoors? Maybe they could go to her house? Perhaps a motel? He would have to pay cash since Carol went through all his credit card bills line by line. God, that woman always complicated things! Any vestige of happiness that had come into his life since their marriage, she found a way to eliminate as if she had radar. Greenblatt wondered if he could bring that point up in couples' therapy but then reconsidered. And now she was threatening to come to choir practice!

Shanna would meet her, see the frump that he married and then call off the whole affair. He couldn't bear it! Greenblatt pulled out his phone and pressed on three, having already keyed Shanna's number there under "Memory."

"Um, Hello?" Shanna said. "Who's this?"

Her voice was so bright and young, Greenblatt almost exploded. "It's me, Raymond. I need.... I really want to see you again. Please?"

There was a long silence in which Greenblatt regretted calling, regretted revealing how desperate he was, when a golden streak of sun cut through the dark storm clouds.

"Me too," he heard Shanna say, and hope filled his heart to the brim.

5. HUNTING AND GATHERING

It pained Farb to leave Elliot with Shanna, but his pitch meeting was being held in Montreal and he was late for his flight. God only knew what political currency had been cashed in by landing CANT's Reality TV Headquarters in Quebec instead of Ontario (where a lion's share of the country's TV production took place), but it must have been worth a bundle. Farb kissed Elliot softly on the cheek and laid him into his crib. They'd done a good share of bonding over the weekend, had covered some important topics (Work, Health, even Religion), and Elliot was reacting more and more—his eyes glittered and he cooed when Farb made a particularly prescient point, his jokes were laughed at appreciatively. Sure Elliot was just a baby, but Farb felt he was really getting through to his five-month old son in a way that would make a lasting impression.

Farb took a quick shower and got himself packed. He tried to avoid Shanna completely but she caught up with him on his way out.

"When will you be back?" she asked, rubbing sleep from her eyes.

"Not to worry, you won't miss choir practice."

"That's not what I asked."

"It's what you meant," Farb said. "Be back tomorrow night after dinner. Don't wait up." Then he walked out the door and into a waiting taxicab, leaving Shanna just annoyed enough not to suspect a thing.

§

Farb didn't check into his hotel until almost midnight. When he got off the elevator his boss, Ari Larson, with his shiny shaved head and ridiculous goatee, was ushering a drunken blonde into his room down the hall. Larson spotted Farb and called out to him obnoxiously: "Don't let me down tomorrow Farb! Maybe jerk off tonight. That always helps *me* relax!" Larson pushed into his room as the blonde giggled "Oh Ari, you are soooooo bad!"

But relaxation never came for Farb. His migraine bullied him all night and when it relented, performance anxiety took over. Once he finally did settle into sleep, a blip lapsed before he woke up in a clammy sweat. His watch had gone missing somewhere in transit between Toronto and Montreal, so he had requested a hotel wake-up call, but it was the hotel alarm clock set for three minutes past seven that roused him. Farb wondered if maybe Larson had cancelled his wake up call. That asshole was famous for hazing his Supervising Producers and he'd love nothing more than to sabotage Farb's big pitch with a prank. Farb needed to stay alert–that's why he'd set the alarm clock as back-up–motto *numero uno*: Just because you're paranoid doesn't mean they're not out to get you.

Farb popped a double dose of migraine meds, showered, shaved and dragged ass downstairs for the free Continental Breakfast with plenty of time to prepare. He was annoyed at how busy it was this early–he was counting on a quiet booth but instead carried his bowl of Raisin Bran and black coffee to a small corner table to rehearse his pitch. "Canadians are masters at the art of apology, and it's time we learn to brag about it." Farb had gold. He just had to keep his cool, lay out the facts that this show would benefit both Canadian culture and more importantly the Network's bottom line, and he'd have a nice little inheritance for Elliot and a big F.U. to Shanna and Toulouse. And if he survived the tumor, well, then he could raise his son with some cushion and… he'd love a Sunday sports car, maybe a Boxster. Farb grinned at the majesty of his coming success, when a waiter asked if he wanted anything from the buffet.

"No, but I'll probably grab some more Raisin Bran," said Farb.

"Oh, cereal isn't part of the buffet," the waiter explained. "We switch up at nine."

"Then I've got plenty of time," Farb said, and went back to his pitch. But when the waiter hovered for just a second too long alarms went off in Farb head. "What time is it exactly?" When the confused waiter hesitated Farb grabbed his wrist. *"SON-OF-A-BITCH!"*

Farb stuffed his bag with documents and rushed past the baffled waiter with flashbulbs exploding in his eyes. *"SON-OF-A-BITCH!"* Out into busy streets of downtown Montreal, Farb elbowed his way through crowds and all but jumped in front of a taxicab. *"Tu es fou?! Maudit Anglais!"* "Just drive!" Screeching through a dozen yellow lights to Place Ville Marie, Farb threw the driver a twenty and ran through the tower's revolving doors. "Come on, come on!" One of the tallest buildings in downtown and three of the five elevators were bust! Sweat poured down Farb's neck, his scalp itched—migraine symptoms crackled. Fuck it. Farb ran for the emergency exit and took the stairs three-by-three, his chest heaving as he made it to five, nine, lungs burning by twelve. By the time he reached the sixteen floor Farb's teeth tingled and he saw stars. Deep breathe Farb. Focus. Stay cool. Deeeeeep breaaaaathe and smiiiiile. Room Sixteen-Twelve....

"Well, if it isn't Mr. Punctuality himself?"

A table with three older men dressed like teenagers and one professionally dressed woman in her late thirties turned their attention from their documents to Farb's pale and disheveled countenance. The men wore Elvis Costello glasses and hipster T-shirts under black leather jackets in a desperate effort to stay relevant for the kids, but all dropped their cool to be annoyed by Farb's tardiness. Still, the most annoyed of all, seemingly livid, was the Senior Vice President of CANT Programming, Jen Rawlings, known to all those who feared her (which was everyone) as Jihad Jen. She bore no resemblance to an Islamic jihadist nor was she even Muslim. She was a slim pale woman with tightly bound hair and enormous green eyes that widened and reddened in rage at the slightest incompetence that had the misfortune of appearing before her. Though her temper was legendary she was known as Jihad Jen for another reason: her "legendary" proclivity for Arab men. The moniker was a cowardly revenge whispered in the steam rooms of sport's clubs by the hoards of men who had been emasculated by Rawlings or anyone who resented her meteoric rise to SVP in only five years. Jihad Jen had once been seen dining in a dimly lit suburban eatery with a man who wore a stylish black and white Palestinian-style *Kafiya,* and that was it. All they had on her was that one sighting, but it was enough for the men to feel they'd grown their balls back, at least until they saw her again.

Farb was doing his best to grow back his own by averting Rawling's withering gaze when an equally sinister but more familiar voice laughed loudly: "Have a seat Farb. Show's almost over!" Larson smiled smugly, sleeves rolled up as if he'd been making deals for hours. "Jesus, you're soaked with sweat!" The men at the table smirked–dressing down a subordinate Producer was all in good fun. Everyone turned back to their documents, but Larson wasn't done. "I just finished telling everyone what an up-and-comer you are, Farb–diligent, ambitious. Then this. You trying to make a liar out of me?"

Farb swallowed hard. "My apologies." He rushed to his seat, coughing loudly, grasping his briefcase like an unopened parachute. "The hotel wake-up call never came."

"No back-up in the electronic age? My clock was set right." Larson shook his head sadly. "I didn't take you for a Luddite, heh-heh...."

"Can we move this along?" Jen Rawlings said, annoyed by the childish bickering. She was more than aware of Larson's reputation as a party-first-work-later type and had no patience for his sadistic sense of humor.

"Of course. Sorry," Larson offered. "As I was saying. If we follow the text on page four. Canadians are a multi-talented people. But our nation's greatest gifts are something that we often apologize for. It's time we learn to brag about our assets. That's why we'd like to pitch out this new great show. Working title: *Canadian Eye For The American Guy!*"

Farb looked down at the pitch document on the table and his stomach dropped. It appeared to be *his* pitch file, but edited to within an inch of its life to make room for Larson's absurdly trite new idea: a fucking makeover show. "Here's where it gets tricky folks...." Farb saw red as Larson continued to hatchet his presentation—a self-congratulatory smile as he read off the lame episode titles, a smug wink as he spoke of integration possibilities, Larson even simulated a baseball player knocking one out of the park as he read the final comments. Farb scanned the table: guys probably with wives and kids, and of course Rawlings. He could see they'd grown bored of Larson's slick arrogance. No matter. Larson had the floor and the esteemed Gordon TV behind him. He'd taken Farb's gold.

"Not bad Ari," Tom Hyde said. "We like the integration opportunities and the Canadian angle. But will people watch it?"

Larson looked over at Farb and smiled. "My second in command Farb here is working on a focus group. He's already done some initial research. Tell them about it, Farb."

All eyes on Farb. In a nanosecond he felt his lungs empty, blood evacuate his brain and heavy sweat soak down his back. "I-I-I...." The room shrunk and the faces around the table grew enormous and ghoulish. "The numbers are, uh, still coming in, uh, but...."

"Forgive my man Farb—not much of a talker," Larson cut in. "What he means is we're still in the process, but the initial response looks good. We'll have the focus group data and of course a fully actualized budget and creative all ready if you like?"

The table of post-hipsters mumbled their approval until the sound of a pen tapping against the table silenced them all. Jihad Jen was about to speak and all eyes turned to the head of the table.

"The idea is extremely weak," Jen Rawlings said, and the men avoided her gaze in shame. "It's a cheap rip off of Queer Eye with none of the edge. Did Gordon actually sign off on this?"

Larson cracked his knuckles and forced a grin, a move that only Farb knew was his tell. "He's on board if you are."

Jihad Jen rolled her eyes. "Look, we all know that Gordon is a friend of CANT—we have a strong history with Gordon TV Productions that means a lot to the network and I have nothing but respect for Gordon. So if he wants this show then we'll consider it. But let me ask you Ari, is this *really* the best you've got?"

All eyes turned to Larson and for the first time his faced showed tension. He glanced nervously over at Farb, shook his own head, and forced another grin. "We have other ideas in the pipeline of course. But I'd hate to pitch you something half-baked especially given the deadline. Why don't you let me send you some paper on...."

"IT'S CALLED *'CANADA'S NEXT GREAT APOLOGIST!'*" Farb blabbed. His voice was high and quaky, a breathy pubescent squeak, but Farb eked it out for a pitch he'd practiced ten thousand times: "The uh, working title is.... It's uh, a show that... well, Canadians are made fun of for apologizing so much, but it's... we could have people compete to be the best at apologizing to, uh, people in their lives and others who deserve one, like, uh First Nations People or uh, Chinese... the Chinese railroad workers... and then, uh, there's comedy and when someone's eliminated they are apologized to. Um that's the, uh, gist for, er, Canada's Next Great Apologist."

When Farb's breath ran out there was a kind of silence in the room that could only be compared to a child's funeral. Larson's head was bowed deeply and the men at the table shot each other worried glances as Rawling's face reddened and her eyes widened to saucers–there was going to be a beheading.

"I apologize Ms. Rawlings," Larson cut in. "Farb here stepped waaay out of line on this one–the idea is clearly nowhere near developed, a real nothing of a pitch...."

"I like it," said Jihad Jen brightly–she almost smiled. The men at the table changed their demeanors immediately–they nodded in agreement, one winked at Farb. "It's different. It's clever, and it's distinctly Canadian."

"Of course, of course," the men said, "Canadian!"

"Might be a bit small," Rawling's continued. "Let's put in some celebrity judges to add some flair, right?"

"Absolutely." Farb scribbled that down, feeling it best not to mention that it was already part of the pitch.

"Has this been cleared with Gordon?"

"I, uh, *mostly,*" Larson said, eyes pinched.

"Good," Jihad Jen said. "Then bring us a full show package for both this and *Canadian Eye.* No problem putting that together in two weeks Ari?"

"Two full show packages in, heh-heh, it's, uh, possible but...."

"Good!" she said. "We have to wrap this up by quarter's end or we might as well kill both ideas. Would be the first time in a while CANT went without a Gordon show on the grid."

"Let's not do that," Larson said very seriously.

"Yes, that would be unfortunate." Rawlings slapped the table. "Let's reconvene in two weeks. We all want something in production before January."

"Same bat time, same bat channel," Farb muttered lamely.

The table collectively flipped their iPads shut and made their way out of the conference room. Larson made sure to shake every hand, comment on hobbies and how hip everyone looked in their vintage T-shirts. When it was just Farb, Larson's smile evaporated. "You. Walk with me. Now."

Farb followed his boss into the elevator. Larson waited until the doors were shut to explode. "YOU ARE SOOOO FUCKING FIRED, FARB! You are sooo—oh! Do you even know what you did in there?!"

"You said I could pitch...."

"Wrong! No! I never said that because—because—it wasn't ready! I read it over and it's missing something. *Canadian Eye* works much, much better."

"You never told Gordon about *The Apologist* did you?" Farb asked.

"Like I said, *The Apologist* isn't ready at all! Gordon's been off golfing in Florida. Why are you even questioning me?"

"You told me he knew about it weeks ago. You lied."

"I'm your fucking boss!" Larson snapped. "And you fucked up big time in there. Two show packages? Do you have have idea how much work that is?! Oh, that cunt! She just looooved saying it, '*Two show packages! Meee-mumu!*' Well, you know what Farb? You dug your own goddamned grave because you're going to get that shit done!"

"What about *The Apologist*?"

"You'll do that too! Alone! Everyone's tied up on the Bruce Cockburn show anyway. And I want every fucking 'I' dotted even if you don't sleep until the meeting or you can pack your shit and find somewhere else to work."

The elevator doors opened and Larson smiled and squeezed Farb's shoulder as they walked through a crowd of colleagues and onto the street. "I just don't get you Farb," Larson said, hailing a cab. "You're thriving at the company. Gordon won't stop talking about what a great ass-kisser you are—he's says you're going to be a big time producer. And you go and do this? What's the fucking rush?"

Farb thought about Elliot, the tumor, Shanna and Greenblatt. "I'm running out of time," he said.

"Then get the fuck to work," Larson ducked into his cab and drove off.

§

Just thinking about the amount of paperwork ahead set off a hailstorm in Farb's skull. Due to CANT's bureaucratic nature their definition of "creating a show package" was a draconian torture applied to anyone unfortunate enough to be in charge of putting the paperwork together. Not only did it mean a fully actualized production budget for a pilot, and then options of six, eight, thirteen and twenty-six episodes, plus a production calendar for two full seasons of each option, but the creative request was lunacy. Most networks asked for only basic episode breakdowns, no more than a paragraph each to start–CANT wanted fully written scripts for each episode, as if the series had already been shot, with Host VO, invented contestant interview bites and fully realized story arcs for the entire season. To do this, one had to sit down and wholly predict the future of a reality TV show. It was CANT's insurance policy–if the show ended up bombing, or in any way deviated from what they wanted, scripts could be pointed to in order to prove that the production company had not delivered what they promised. It was a near-Sisyphean task that a team of producers was generally given a solid month to accomplish. Farb had twelve days and he was doing it all alone. A stress migraine half-blinded him through the flight back to Toronto and worsened upon landing.

And yet on the cab ride home a strange pride rose up in Farb, making him giddy. The pitch had been a sloppy mess, yes–his breath had abandoned him despite all of his prep. But he'd pushed through. *The Apologist* was alive, and Elliot still had a chance! For a moment Farb allowed himself to forget his illness, Greenblatt, and relent fully to the joy of success. He looked out the window at his neighborhood and admired the rows of sleepy suburban homes with their quaint faux-cobblestone driveways, basketball hoops and hissing sprinklers. Farb had done well in providing for Shanna and Elliot so far, had moved them somewhere safe and green, and had done it with his own sweat.

"I'm going to be rich!" Farb said, handing the cabbie a ten-dollar tip.

"Thanks, Bro. Me too!"

And as Farb was left alone in front of his house he had an overwhelming urge to urinate on his flower garden. He did and it felt fantastic.

§

Shanna heard the front door open and quickly hung up the phone. She'd been talking to her mother, not telling her but not-not telling her either–she hinted that she had met a man, that he was a nice man, a doctor, that they took a nice walk. She wanted her mother to tell her that it was okay, that she was allowed an indiscretion in a marriage like hers, but before her mother could react Shanna was forced to hang up. She jumped into bed quickly, grabbed a gossip magazine and flipped to the "Fat Or Flat" section at the back.

"I'm hoo-oome!" Farb called out.

Shanna didn't budge. She tensed up as Farb entered the bedroom and winced when he dropped his bags at the foot of the bed like a soldier back from war.

"Just sat down for the first time today," Shanna complained by way of greeting. "Chicken's in the fridge with rice–just heat it up in the microwave."

"That's the kind of welcome I get?" Farb arched his eyebrow. "How about 'Honey, I'm so glad to have you back. Thank you for slaving away late into the night so that our family can eat?'"

"Look I'm exhausted, okay? I just put Elliot down. Can't you see I'm emptying my brain?"

"Sorry to interrupt. Would you at least come down? A king shouldn't dine alone."

Shanna sighed. "You know what? Fine." She slapped down the magazine and hurled off her blankets like trash. "I'll keep working."

Farb grinned as Shanna stomped down the stairs. So she's going to continue to mask her deception with martyrdom? How imaginative and self-serving. But Farb knew he had to be careful for a while. It would behoove him to keep things relatively contentious with Shanna, because if things blew up and the truth spilled out he would be sidetracked from his work and from spending time alone with Elliot. He had to stay cool. Keep things as normal and fucked up as possible.

Shanna pulled a plate of chicken and rice out of the microwave and dropped it on the table. Farb unfolded a napkin on his lap.

"Tomorrow's a six o'clock practice to prepare for Sukkot," Shanna said when Farb was served. "So I need you to come home early to watch Elliot."

"Not a problem," said Farb, but tried not to sound happy about it. "If this weekend was any indication, providing childcare isn't as hard as you let on. I've got a pretty light workload this week. Maybe I can even bring Elliot to the office for an hour or so a day."

"A lot of parents bring their children to the office all day," Shanna informed him, playing right into Farb's hands. "That would be a normal job."

"Yeah, but I actually work during the day."

"And I don't?" Shanna snapped. "What do you think?!"

"Fine," Farb sighed. "I'll take him all morning tomorrow and even all day. I'll bring the Pack n' Play and some toys. In fact I'll take him all week, how about that? It will be an experiment. That way you'll have more time to shop and do Pilates."

"Oh fuck you! Look I cooked and served you. Can I go upstairs now?"

"Aren't you going to ask me what happened on my trip? I mean I was out there half way around the world trying to put food on the table."

"It's an hour flight. Look who's being dramatic now?"

"This concerns you too, Shanna," Jonathan said, knowing he had her. "If this show gets green lit it could mean a promotion. And if I get a promotion that means more money. More money for the family. For you. A nicer house. A better life. For you. You. You. You. How can I make this abstraction more clear? More shopping money for your Ebay shoe fetish?"

"Oh fuuuuuck you!" Shanna threw up her hands. "You know what? I'm done. Goodnight!"

Farb slammed down his fork with a dramatic flair and pushed back his chair. Shanna stormed off upstairs and slammed the bedroom door. In seconds she was back on the phone with her mother.

§

Farb washed the dishes and left a Post-it note reading: "I washed these." Then he walked up to Elliot's room, creaking open the door slowly. He picked the baby out of the crib and held him against his chest. The weight of him, the drool he oozed onto Farb's shirt momentarily washed everything away.

"We can do this," Farb whispered, kissing Elliot's forehead. "You and me, kid."

6. THE SWITCH

As requested by his wife, Raymond Greenblatt picked up a quarter pound of organic cottage cheese and went into Shopper's Drugmart to grab her crazy pills. It had been two years since the girls went off to university and Carol went on a steady dose of anti-anxiety medication. And thank God for it! Empty Nest Syndrome is no joke, Greenblatt learned, and it didn't end when the girls came home for their quarterly visits. Carol had always been a busybody, perpetually anxious about little things, but after the girls moved out, "new-onset agoraphobia" (Latin for "busybodyitis") reinforced her fixations. Unmedicated for the first months Carol barely got out of the house for more than groceries and always had an excuse to stay at home. Housework is endless, the yard needs weeding, something historic is on TV. On the rare occasion they did have somewhere to go together socially Greenblatt would settle himself on the couch all dressed and watch the History Channel while Carol made endless wardrobe changes ("Are these earrings too old for me?"). More often than not it ended in a meltdown and by the time she eventually did get dressed it was too late. At first Greenblatt suspected it was all a power play. She would keep him waiting to control him, but all the signs pointed to a larger problem. So he arranged an appointment with one of the hospital psychiatrists and Carol was given a prescription.

The medication helped. Carol became functional, even happy, but as far as Greenblatt could tell her intensity persisted and grew even more focused. Now instead of floundering between tasks, Carol centered her manic energy towards efficiency and specifically filling the void left by her departed daughters. So she concentrated on down her list: her marriage. This coping strategy changed Greenblatt's life and not for the better. He watched as his wife conducted telephone interviews with dozens of couples' therapists, marriage counselors and new age relationship coaches from the "Wave Foundation Couples Retreat" to "Healthy Colonic, Happy Couple Fest." Not until she was absolutely certain that she'd found the right one–cheap and close–did she finally settle. When Greenblatt arrived to therapy with Carol he found himself face to face with her clone–fifty-something, Jewish, and maybe even a little more dedicated to testicle removal.

However, the first session went surprisingly well. When asked about his childhood, Greenblatt choked up, getting into the whole story about his father and his father's "friend" Minka. Was this all they wanted? A few tears and he was off the hook? Greenblatt would more than willingly emasculate himself weekly if it meant stuffing a sock in his wife's pie-hole. That the therapist would express shock and outrage at Greenblatt's slightest revelation ("My mother never hugged me") made it easy for him to feel empathy and let his emotions run wild. Couples' therapy seemed to be a breeze, forty-five minutes on the couch and home free for the week. But Greenblatt had miscalculated severely. In his effort to please, he had divulged all too soon, and when there was nothing self-abasing left to reveal he had to confront hard, cruel analysis. After only a few sessions, instead of welcoming Greenblatt's emotional openness as they had done, the evil twins began to dissect him one particle of testosterone at a time. Then, armed with x-rays he had given them, it was as if they had been planning radical emergency surgery all along, waiting patiently to cut off his balls when he was tied to the operating table with his own rope. "Don't you see that your parents' divorce and the rejection that came with your father's emotional abandonment has left you with deep scars that you are trying to heal by punishing Carol?" accused the therapist triumphantly. Greenblatt had somehow forgotten what women really do when faced with male vulnerability: punish it. They nit picked his faults, scoffed at his contributions to the family (as for the value of man's work and his steady paycheck, it was brushed aside other than to imply that he used it for control and punishment). When Greenblatt tried to defend himself by describing late nights at the hospital tending to sick patients, the response he got from the therapist was, "So you admit to only doing one thing? You escape to work and that's all. Are you aware of all the many different things Carol does? Just how much is on her plate? No, I didn't think so...." Then Carol began, in their fifth session, to reveal trifling tidbits about their marriage. In a hushed tone when she told the stunned therapist that Greenblatt had once called her a "controlling cunt," well that—that—became the focus of a month of sessions. His aggression, "male aggression" as the therapist called, it was pathological and had to stop before someone got seriously hurt. The therapist meant Carol of course but Greenblatt understood it to mean him or at least it felt that way as the two women took turns pummeling him in a Kafkaesque twist where he had to pay for the privilege of being repeatedly emasculated by Carol times two. What Greenblatt needed was quite simple—for Carol to chill out again. Not be so frenetic. Stay home like she did when the girls left for school. Not show up to choir practice, not borrow his blue binder and memorize the Hebrew verses as if to taunt him with the inevitability of her arrival. But again (and again) Carol was determined to interfere. She was a leech drawing his very lifeblood. He needed this affair with Shanna, needed it to live.

Well, he wouldn't let Carol end it. Couldn't. Shanna had become too important to him. So when he walked up to the medicine counter at Shopper's Drugmart and paid for his wife's meds, he also picked up a bottle of Vitamin C, which he replaced for Carol's pills in the parking lot. Agoraphobia may be an unpleasant condition but it sure eased some of the fear of getting caught *in delicto* with your mistress. And maybe the vitamins would put some color in her face.

7. WORK

Farb's first few days back at the office consisted, equally, of paperwork and childcare. While Elliot slept near his desk or played with the magnetized alphabet blocks he'd brought from home, Farb soldiered on, writing up dozens of story summaries and getting started on the calendars. Shanna called every couple of hours and Farb assured her that Elliot was "perfectly happy." He'd set up an entire nursery, complete with crib and changing station. Farb condescendingly assured his cheating heart: "You need your rest. You haven't slept since before you were pregnant. Time to focus on yourself for a while."

Meanwhile Farb pushed forward on the *Canadian Eye* documents, racing to where he could focus on *The Apologist*. Having Elliot in the office provided Farb the perfect excuse to keep his office door shut most of the day. The one time Larson had burst in to check up on *Canadian Eye,* he caught one glimpse of Elliot's diarrhea-smeared butt cheeks and gagged his way back out. No one else bothered him, and those who needed Farb knew to knock first.

A little less easy to avoid were the calls that came in from Dr. Arupal urging Farb to begin immediate treatment for his brain tumor. It was a daily reminder that time was limited. Treatment had to begin quickly, Arupal explained, as Farb's chances were diminishing by the day. Act now or risk certain death, that was his choice. But Farb would be damned if he was going to spend his last days hooked up to chemo, losing his strength and dignity, too helpless to work on his pitch and bond with Elliot. So the calls persisted and Farb kept his focus on the office.

Still, Farb realized that if he was going to raise Elliot right, he needed to get more proactive than just pre-recording lectures and writing letters for posterity. It would mean a few field trips. Farb still hadn't crossed Education off his list since his duty was to make sure that Elliot got the best available start. Access to the top schools was the most important thing and Shanna couldn't be trusted with the task of researching through the competing claims. Her hippie brother Jeffrey had attended the Ginsberg Cooperative and she always bragged about how creative and happy he was as a result.

Jeffrey was a fucking mooch and a dope peddler. Farb would be damned if his son was going to forgo reading and math class to flit around a classroom in a fairy costume building felt castles all day. So Farb got to work, making some aggressive moves over the week that he hoped would ensure his son's eventual admission to Harvard.

And, as he strolled across the campus of The Canadian Royal Pacific Pre-Kindergarten Academy, Elliot strapped to his chest in a pink Baby Bjorn, Farb knew he'd made the right decision. It was a crisp day; the sun sparkled on the granite steps of Pacific Manor. A podium displaying the school's crest (two crossed silver spoons, set against the backdrop of the TSE) had been set up next to the soccer field. A golden shovel had been artfully set in a pile of dirt and a shiny red ribbon was tied between two newly planted birch trees. The small crowd that settled into padded folding chairs consisted of teachers and parents on the school's elite board. Most were dressed up for the occasion—Brooks Brothers suits for the men and Channel hats for the women. Farb walked over and shook hands with the Principal, O'Conner, and posed for a newsletter photo-op.

"Lovely day to break ground," O'Conner said through a frozen smile.

"Nice day for an acceptance letter too," Farb reminded him.

"Unusual circumstances. Extra channels. But rest assured your son will be admitted once the check clears."

"All I need to know."

The two men tightened their grips and gave extra hard pats on the back, then O'Conner stepped to the podium and looked out on the crowd of tight-lipped Wasps with a smile. "Faculty, parents, members of the Board of Trustees, dear friends. We are gathered here today to witness a milestone not only in the history of this esteemed learning institution but also in the Canadian Education system as a whole."

Farb stood nearby waiting to simply cut the ceremonial ribbon. Normally a speech from the benefactor would be in order, but Farb insisted the ceremonial speech be delivered by the Principal. But as he stood there squeezing Elliot's hand, something gnawed at him. Farb's fear of drooling in public while he tried to pronounce the word "matriculate" was real, yet here was an opportunity for him to face his fears and teach Elliot in the process. This was a low-stress engagement, a forgiving crowd–even if he stumbled at least he tried. And Elliot would see it all–remember the smiling crowd and feel calmed by it as an adult. Farb needed to break the cycle and he needed to do it now.

"Principal, if you wouldn't mind," Farb cut in. "I'd like to say a few words." The Principal gave Farb an odd look–it wasn't what they'd discussed, but he then stepped aside with an ingratiating smile motioning to the crowd to appreciate the speaker.

Farb swallowed hard. It was one thing to think about it and another thing to face the crowd. Hollowness formed in his chest and he felt his palms tingle. Farb closed his eyes, kissed Elliot's head and inhaled his sweet butterscotch.

"I could go on for days lauding the significance of this grand step," Farb began, his voice cracking only a bit, "but a recent study suggests that during a public speech the audience pays attention to only ten percent of what the speaker is actually saying and the other ninety percent have sexual fantasies about the other people in attendance, so I'll be brief."

It was old joke, an opener he'd heard in a pitch and it warranted a yelp of disapproval from the Head of Fundraising, Kristin Schiff.

But Farb quickly whispered an apology and continued: "A little back-story if you would allow me—I can tell you first hand that arriving at this moment was not easy. Merely convincing the current administration to entertain the idea was an exercise in artful persuasion. My proposal was met with disdain at worst and, at the best, vicious hostility. 'They're far too young!' the Board argued. Still, by the end of my impassioned plea they came around and I applaud their vision. After all, bringing this project to fruition took wisdom, it took commitment, it took steely nerve. But most of all it took cold hard cash. My cold hard cash." Farb took a nice pause there. He was rolling and Elliot giggled. "To get the Board on board, so to speak, I agreed to have an architect flown in from Denmark to develop an ergonomic swing set; the contents of a sandbox will be hypo-allergenic sand imported from a beach on the Polynesian Island of Tuvalu. The teak see-saw is being shipped from Uruguay in a 'Fair Trade' pact that, while making no sense economically, warmed the hearts of the more liberal members of the planning committee, particularly former Greenpeace Canada Vice-Chairman Jake Reilly." The Reillys nodded appreciatively. "The full expense of this facility matched with a generous contribution to Royal Pacific's 'Capital Improvement Campaign' gifted in part with the two thousand dollar diamond earrings that I 'won' at the charity auction and you're starting to get the picture of the magnitude of my financial commitment here."

"You might wonder why anyone would go to such extremes merely to ensure that their child matriculates at a private pre-kindergarten? Surely there is a less costly route. I have my reasons. The same reasons that account for the near biblical exodus to private schools all over the country: The pathetic alternative. Canadian public schools are a modern Babylon of liberal decerebrates run by a cabal of shaggy bearded bureaucrats who are useless—worse—who are destructive to the process of educating our nation's youngest. 'Open Classrooms'? 'Mixed Ability Grades'? 'Invented Spelling'? 'Gender Neutral Learning'—and no tests! How do you expect these kids to have any sense of accomplishment let alone shame? Academic experts claim the focus of education has shifted from hard sciences to teaching children how to advocate for themselves, but if these kids were taught to read rather than how to build a village with paper maché they would advocate loud and clear: 'Mom, Dad. Give me a chance in life!'" Farb scanned the crowd—many shifted uncomfortably, more stared in disbelief. Elliot cackled. "Socrates once said that an education obtained with money is no education at all. Socrates never had to send his kid to City Pre-K. The Canadian government has squandered our tax dollars and left us with no choice but to eschew the whole public system and succumb to extortion. Which is the reason why we are all here today." Farb held up an enormous pair of golden scissors and approached the red ribbon. "May I present to you The Farb Pre-MBA Jungle Gym and GMAT-Prep Facility." There was a soupçon of applause accompanied by rigorous clapping from Judy Sands, the head of Royal Pacific's Ethical Fundraising Committee. "Education is a most subjective thing. To a young child a sandbox is merely a sandbox, an opportunity to build castles and maybe see how deep they can dig. But what if by some rare geographical phenomenon the child digs very deep and strikes oil? How then will they manage? There's international distribution to think about, drilling, pipelines to build, OPEC to contend with. My goal here, ladies and gentlemen, is to educate our children towards that possibility. To ensure that our nation's youngest develop into contributing members of society in the highest tax bracket. Forgive the pun, but The Farb Pre-MBA Jungle Gym is a giant leap in instilling the capitalist instinct into the curious minds of Royal Pacific Academy's youngest students. Not to mention–slides are fun." Farb looked out to the crowd again–some had begun to leave in disgust, and he felt his time was running out. "Thank you very much and enjoy the future."

There was another attempt at applause as Farb left the podium. The Reillys were rounding the crowd to congratulate him, but there was no time to schmooze. Farb had money to make. He had laid down a chunk of savings to make this happen and it was time to get back to work and refill the family coffers. But the speech had gone well, he sensed Elliot had learned a valuable lesson in courage today, and Farb could check another lesson off the list.

8. DALLIANCE

When Greenblatt pulled into the parking lot at Temple Beth-El he was plagued by thoughts of death and drowning. He told himself his affair with Shanna was a "transitory fling"—a dalliance, and that she was only meeting him to end it. He felt a strong instinct to drive away fast, hide in his basement with his antique pistols—at least he'd have the memory of his time with the lovely bird and a generous deposit to the wank bank. He circled the parking lot and was about to pull off when he saw her walking along the side of the synagogue.

"I was afraid you wouldn't come," he said.

"I parked around the corner," Shanna said. "If we're going to continue to do this, we should be discreet."

Deep in the ravine was a small wooden supplies shed overgrown with leaves and moss. It was used only on weekends, a rest stop for the Equestrian Center. Greenblatt scoped it out and decided it was a perfect love nest—weatherproof, off the walking path, and far enough from synagogue parking that they could not be spotted or sniffed out as they puffed away. The only downside was the smell of horse manure, which Greenblatt suppressed with scented candles. For Greenblatt keeping the mood sexy was key, and he didn't want any distractions from savoring every scent and sensation. He set up a mirror next to the blanket so that he could be sure it was all really happening. Obviously if it continued they would go to hotels but, for now, this was more exciting.

Shanna enjoyed the lovemaking, but looked forward to Greenblatt's quality weed even more. Shanna would get so high she could almost imagine she wasn't with Greenblatt at all—that she was back at McGill with one of the male cast-mates in her art troupe *Les Terribles,* the tempestuous young men with shoulder-length hair and a passion for "Post Structuralist Monologue."

While Greenblatt and Shanna were making it like hippies backstage at a Phish concert, Carol Greenblatt prepared herself to drive to Temple Beth-El for her first choir practice in ages. It had been a good two years since she'd quit the choir and so it was important she return looking her best. Earrings would be an issue. The outfit she laid out would require a nice set, and it took a while to think about which would match best. When she finally chose, she remembered that she had left that particular pair of earrings at her sister's house in Mississauga. She should call–get her to stick them in the mail–maybe overnight them, or maybe she should drive to Mississauga right then and get them? But then she would be far too late for choir practice and that would defeat the whole purpose. Maybe her red blouse and long gold chain would do? The blouse had gold lamé on the fringes and the necklace would pull it together. She scanned her closet, found an appropriate jacket right away, but struggled to find the blouse until she looked in the laundry bin. And there it was, a bit wrinkled from trying it on the previous day but not technically dirty. She would just shake it and give it a quick iron. Only problem was that the last time she'd tried the blouse on she was wearing a different perfume and her hypersensitive nose wouldn't be able to handle the mix of scents. Oh, and look at this laundry basket–full to the brim! She'd better not let it stew. She sifted through the basket and separated whites from colors, finding clothes she'd tried on only to reject, when amongst the garments she found a pair of Raymond's pants–the worn-out green corduroys that were his favorite. She wasn't sure why he wore them, they made him look grandfather-ish and were ill fitting around the groin, but Raymond was never one to look fashionable. "What in the world?" She held the pants up to the light and saw a yellowish dirt stain. Again? She held it up to her nose and it was unmistakable. Horse manure and of course little whiffs of marijuana (her husband's little adolescent hobby). Geez! Had they not fixed the door at the synagogue yet? This was just ridiculous. She had half a mind to call them up and threaten to dial the fire department for breaking code if they didn't fix it. And why should Ray always be the hero and soil his pants? Having horses so nearby a house of prayer had to be a health code infraction of some sort and was *traif* to boot–shouldn't they at least be forced to poop and scoop? She couldn't bear it. She lay down Ray's pants and grabbed for the spray and wash but found it empty. Dammit! It was on her shopping list and that list needed to get done, but there were so many things to accomplish what with cleaning, baking, bills and other odds and ends that she hadn't gotten out. But tonight was different. So she would miss this week's choir practice? There was always next week. And by then she would have her sister mail those earrings over. Tonight Carol's big trip would be to the grocery store where she could be useful and wear comfortable sweatpants. "More comfortable, anyway." Carol retrieved the pills Raymond picked up for her at Shopper's and popped two, then visited each room in the house to make sure the lights were off. She double-checked that the oven hadn't been left on since she baked that banana bread (major fire hazard–was their fire insurance updated?), lowered the thermostat (why waste money warming an empty house?), and checked the phone messages just in case the girls called. Finally she made it out to the car. It was just after dusk and she wondered if Raymond would be home soon. She wanted to discuss the possibility of hosting their therapy sessions at the house–Fran had already agreed to it and she could serve the banana bread.

On the drive to Loblaws, Carol put the radio on very low. She wanted to make sure to hear any sirens especially ones headed to her house (had she made certain to turn off the oven?). –But loud enough so that she could hear the news of any road accidents. She stopped at a gas station on a whim and decided to call her daughters, neither of whom picked up, but she left messages for both explaining that she was, "Just out and about." She wasn't sure why but she felt pride in saying that phrase "just out and about!" The girls worried, so they should know where she was just in case they called. As Carol merged back on the road, she reflected that her daughters probably think she's gone a bit kooky in her old age, just like their grandmother had been in her later years. Well, wait until they raise teenage girls! That's what her own mom said and look at her now! Carol always thought she would become more confident and daring with age, but instead there was so much more to worry about, so much more at stake. At least she wasn't reacting as drastically as Raymond. In midlife Raymond had regressed to adolescence. He collected silly war antiques, grew that ridiculous beard, and of course there was his little habit of smoking marijuana which stunk up all his clothes. He said "like" more often, would wonder aloud "if Socialism was given a fair shake." Weed was used to relax and as an aphrodisiac–she felt like Raymond's interest in smoking again might be some kind of mating ritual. He had been more amorous lately, squeezing her at night in bed, but he'd taken an adolescent spin on sex too, brazenly requesting oral sex from her or covering her face with a pillow when they made love as if to get kinky.

Yes, his behavior was unusual lately, but who was she to talk? It took her hours to get out of the house just for groceries.

In the parking lot of Loblaws, some idiot had straddled the last two good spots. Carol had a mind to write "Learn To Park!" in lipstick on his windshield since she heard that it was almost impossible to get lipstick off glass, but instead she found a spot way off in the corner and legged it across the lot. Carol's mood brightened as she strode the well-lit aisles inside. She just loved how organized it was—so methodical, clean and intuitive. The cans and produce arranged just so. No mess. In Aisle F she found the heavy-duty cleaner right where it was supposed to be and On Special. For deep dirt and stains. Oh, Raymond that little monkey! She placed the detergent in her cart and walked on, adding a few other cleaning products until she was satisfied that she was double-stocked on everything. Never again would she be caught with her pants down! Though she only had nine items, Carol skipped the Express line, too disgusted was she by the presence of a young man who was trying to sneak in fifteen items. Probably the same guy who double-parked. Jerk. Who could stand it? Carol instead took her place in a regular line behind a woman with only seven items and she liked that—why take the easy way out? Besides, the woman, who had lovely black curls that reminded her of her youngest daughter Beth, was buying diapers. It made her miss her girls when they were babies. Carol peeked deeper into the woman's cart and saw that she was also buying formula. She felt a tinge of empathy for the young woman. Unable to feed her own child! Carol used to love taking Beth and Jennifer to her breast, being able to give them the best directly from her body. She was certain there would be less of a connection between them if she hadn't. How could a baby even tell the difference between mother and father, and how sad it would have been if the girls took to Raymond instead of her? Carol caught a glimpse of the woman's face—she was beautiful though sad, so Carol was sure that they were on the same page about breastfeeding. As Carol watched, the woman unloaded her items onto the counter so absentmindedly that she didn't notice that one of her cans of formula had white crust on the edges and had clearly been tampered with. Carol was about to say something when she also noticed a blue choir binder poking out of the woman's purse, the ubiquitous blue binder from Temple Beth-El.

"You might want to replace that one," Carol said to the woman, with a gentle smile. "One of your formula cans has been opened. If you hold my place in line, I know exactly where they are."

"Oh, that's kind of you," Shanna blushed, trying to snap herself out of whatever daydream she was caught in.

Carol bounced off to Aisle K next to the cereals and made a speedy return with a new can. "I made sure this one was sealed," she said, handing Shanna the jar. "You can never be too careful. You read so many horrible stories these days."

"I appreciate it, really."

"We moms should stick together. Mine are off at university now. It's cliché beyond words but they do grow up fast. How old is yours? I assume at your age you have only one so far."

"Almost six months. A boy."

"Well he must trust his dad to be away from his mother right now. My girls used to scream bloody murder if I left them alone for even an hour. I had to sit in their room until they would nap. 'Attachment Parenting' indeed, heh-heh."

Shanna felt a tinge of guilt redden her face so she just nodded and went back to watching her items get keyed in. Carol intuited that she had brought up an uncomfortable subject so she shifted gears. It wasn't often she met a nice woman at the grocery store she felt was so easy to talk to.

"I don't mean to pry," she went on. "But are you by any chance in the choir at Temple Beth-El? I recognize the blue binder. I was a member for several years before I quit. Couldn't make it out that late and still cook dinner for the girls. I was actually planning on going back tonight, but obviously the day passed. Sounds like such a bother the way my husband describes it. Why don't they fix that door? It's why I'm here getting detergent."

"The door's broken? I didn't know."

"Oh, my husband's always on his hands and knees trying to get in through the window. Mud stains right through the knees."

"I'm often late," Shanna muttered, feeling her body tense up.

"Oh, I'm sorry–I'm Carol. My husband is Ray–with the goofy beard. Not much of a singer but he just loves it. You must have met."

"Paper or plastic Miss?" the clerk asked.

"Huh?"

"Plastic?"

"Oh, uh plastic–yes–it's fine."

"Do you know him?" Carol asked.

"Um, I don't think he, uh, sounds familiar." Shanna's face filled with color as she fumbled in her purse. Her hands shook as she handed the clerk a wad of bills.

"Well I'm Carol Greenblatt. I didn't catch your name?"

"Oh, um, Shanna. Uh, Farb. I'm Shanna Farb." The clerk handed Shanna her change, more than half the money she had handed him in the first place and Shanna tucked it messily in her purse. "Thanks for the uh, the uh, formula–thanks."

"It's nothing, really. Well Shanna, I look forward to seeing you in choir practice soon!"

"Right," Shanna squirmed, and quickly scurried off.

Carol watched the strange young woman bump her cart into a pyramid display of mouthwash as she raced out the door.

"Odd bird," Carol remarked to the grocery clerk who just shrugged. "Seemed to be in a real hurry all of the sudden."

Carol began unloading when, somewhere between the paper towels and the chicken thighs, Shanna's familiarity dawned upon her. It wasn't the black curly hair that was so similar to her daughter's, or even the strange coincidence of her blue choir binder that reminded the woman to her. It was the smell. Carol's hypersensitive nose told her everything she couldn't piece together when Shanna was in front of her. It was a faint smell but it was there—the same one that had led her to the grocery store in the first place. To buy heavy-duty detergent. It was the same smell on her husband. The exact same smell of marijuana and horseshit.

9. MIRACLES

Farb danced around his office twirling Elliot in the air and making muffler sounds with his lips. Airborne, Elliot squealed with delight as a sofa landing ended in a dozen belly kisses. It was exhausting, but Farb enjoyed playing with Elliot for a good while each day, singing to him, encouraging him to crawl or tossing him in the air. The baby responded joyfully to the physical fun and Farb was sure Elliot was going to be some kind of athlete, able to bench his father one day. But while he was still little, Farb could do what he wanted and even humiliate him a bit. So he'd gotten in the habit of dressing the baby up in a tie and taking photos of him doing adult things like sipping from a coffee mug or using a calculator. He drew a sign: "The Poop Stops Here!" and sat Elliot next to it in a big office chair. Ridiculous Facebook fodder but Elliot humored him, hamming it up for the camera like a pro. And since it was well known that Farb was plagued with the impossible task of preparing two show packages for The Network all alone, he was left to do whatever absurdity he wanted. The crazier Farb acted the more people avoided him, in fact assuming that he was cracking under pressure. In truth, Farb was just getting used to the art of parenthood. He had improved his change-and-feed process to a four minute pit stop but had also been wise enough to hire some partial childcare in his office, an empathetic woman named Margie who came in for a few hours each day to play with Elliot while Farb worked. Margie never asked about Farb's peculiar habit of working under low lights or with a wet towel over his forehead and that suited Farb just fine. His headaches were constant, far less responsive to pills, and he squinted at the computer screen and often saw double. One day, when the pain seemed unbearable, Farb responded to one of Dr. Arupal's calls. He paid an uncomfortable visit to her office in which she scolded him and then almost begged him to enter treatment immediately. But mercifully she prescribed some higher strength painkillers and suggested cold compresses that performed miracles in taking pressure off Farb's temples.

"You can't run forever," Dr. Arupal warned. "Things are becoming irreversible."

Late at night Farb snacked on peanuts, leftover Chinese, and burnt coffee with creamer. While the office bustled during the day it was empty at night and the steady buzz of florescent lights and the misplaced desire to steal office supplies kept him company. In terms of actual human interaction there were only a few interruptions: the janitorial staff, who entered Farb's office to unload his garbage regardless of how engrossed Farb was or how lightly Elliot slept; Sid, the octogenarian security guard who performed a military salute every night at midnight; and of course there was Alicia Gordon, Gordon's spoiled and flirtatious teenage daughter to contend with. Known to most of the producers as "Office Jailbait," Alicia came to the office most nights to "study for her SATs" in a quiet environment. Her father bragged how Alicia's "knack for bitchiness" pointed to a lucrative career in litigation. He promised to pay for a trip to Amsterdam with all of her friends if she made it into a reputable American school, and, with his connections, she was a shoo-in so long as she scored mid-range. But Alicia's books never got cracked. Instead she video chatted with her Parisian boyfriend and took hits from her marijuana vaporizer, which she nicknamed "Vapey." When she wasn't communing with Vapey, she was taunting her father's employees who she knew were helpless to retaliate. Farb was far from immune. On one particular mid-week night after some hearty partying Alicia stumbled drunk down the hall and stood in front of Farb's open office door.

"Another late night, Big Daddy? Your wife must get lonely."

"So must your SAT books," Farb replied.

Alicia flipped him off, "My father will demote you to Siberia if he knew you were even talking to me. And don't think he's impressed by all your late nights—I told him all you do is surf gay porn and jerk it!"

The only others who often roamed the halls late at night and could be heard debating the value of various 1980s comedies were Raj and Rahul Nehru, cleverly known around the office as the Nehru Brothers. Despite their East Indian names, the Nehru Brothers were about as Waspy as you get—golf-shirted, Starbucks-swilling, round-faced and doughy like two little Stay Puft Marshmallow Men. And they were Wasps: they owed their names to their father, a sitar-playing hippie from Halifax who converted to Hinduism after seeing Ravi Shankar perform at the Monterey Pop Festival in '67. The Brothers, who inherited none of their father's musical abilities but retained enough intelligence to be grateful their father wasn't a fan of Sha Na Na, had been hired right out of Humber College's New Media program. Their hire at the firm was a no-brainer—the Brothers graduated top of their class, but it was their status as presumed minorities that made it easy and allowed them to phone in their interviews. As a longtime partner of the CANT, Gordon TV Productions was asked to abide by its "Excellence in Diversity" campaign and the Nehru's would be perfect poster boys. Their first day on the job was a planned paparazzi frenzy of brochure photo-ops for the firm's Quarterly Newsletter. But when Raj and Rahul showed up and it became clear that they weren't "ethnic in any way shape or form," the Human Resources Representative responsible for recruiting them (and passing over a much more presentable Jamaican woman who just happened to be a single mother) was fired on the spot. To avoid a lawsuit, the Brothers were retained as Junior Development Executives, which meant they were put in charge of night logging and if they weren't busy after that, office mail distribution. The Brothers were told they could work together so long as they worked odd hours, and they agreed so long as they were also allowed to wear surf shorts and ironic T-shirts to work, which they did with great consistency. Over the past months Farb bumped into them often late at night and they had taken a shine to Elliot, sometimes bringing him toys based on their obscure eighties film fetish. It was during one of Farb's late nights that the Brothers stumbled into Farb's office squabbling passionately about two classics of modern cinema.

"Dead wrong. *Ruthless People* is a far superior to *Soapdish*–Judge Reinhold alone made it into a masterpiece, not to mention Danny DeVito and Bette Midler," insisted Raj.

"*Soapdish* had two-time Academy Award nominee Robert Downey Jr. and early Elizabeth Shue! And let's please not forget the best role of Whoopi Goldberg's life not including when she dated Ted Danson," argued Rahul.

"What's that's supposed to mean? They were a good couple!"

"It was a media ploy! And even if they were really dating, that whole blackface debacle was a desperate plea for help."

"Love does funny things to people."

They opened Farb's office door with his mail in hand and found Farb lying on the couch looking dazed and spookily pale. "Michael Keaton in *Beetlejuice*," Raj said.

"Shut it, Raj," Rahul said. "Oh, sorry Mr. Farb. We didn't know you were still around."

Farb looked up, eyes sunken from sleep deprivation. "Come on in guys. More bills?"

"Junk. But I brought something awesome for Elliot."

"*We* brought," Rahul said, annoyed. "Why does it always have to be about you? I was the one who found it online. Just because you picked it up at the Can-Pop conference...."

"It's a George Carlin doll! From *Outrageous Fortune* with Shelley Long and a whole bunch of Indian tribesmen. See the ponytail?"

"Can we give it to him now?"

"I'm afraid he's asleep, guys," said Farb.

"Well, maybe we can just leave it next to his crib. He can wake up to it. He'll be psyched!" Raj placed the vintage doll next to Elliot's crib.

"Thoughtful. Thanks guys."

"You're the only one who really talks to us around here," said Rahul, "and Elliot's the coolest. We should start him in on the pure genius of *Soapdish* as soon as possible."

"Despite its inferiority to *Ruthless People.*"

Farb got up from the couch. "Time to get back to work."

"Mr. Farb, are you going crazy like everyone in the office is saying?" asked Raj.

"Raj!" Rahul pushed his brother. "None of your business!"

"Sorry."

"No, no–it's fine. I wish I could give you a straight answer. Might be. It's complicated, I can say that."

The Nehru's laid down Farb's mail and walked out and Farb could hear Rahul reprimanding his brother for asking stupid questions. But how stupid was it really? Maybe Farb was going insane? Dr. Arupal warned him that his behavior would be erratic due to the placement of the tumor. Maybe he was just leading himself to the psych ward. Hell, maybe he was already in a psych ward and none of this even existed and he was just rocking in a padded cell in a straight jacket covered in his own feces? That would make things less complicated. Despite that possibility, Farb pushed on with his work for Elliot's sake, and for what was left of his sanity. He focused on the budget numbers, but soon his eyes blurred up and he fell asleep face down on his desk.

Two hours later Farb's head was bitten right off his neck. He was sailing around the Greek Islands with Elliot and two beautiful mermaids–sun glimmered on their pert young breasts as they dipped their glittering tails in the warm ocean water when a swarm of hungry sharks descended on them, devouring the mermaids and chewing through the hull of the boat like cardboard. Farb trod blood-soaked water holding Elliot above his head–he could feel the sharks circle, when God's voice boomed: "Mr. Farb? Mr. Farb? Are you awake? The baby is crying. Mr. Farb?"

"Mr. Farb? Mr. Farb? Are you awake? The baby is crying."

Farb burst out of sleep to find the Brothers hovering over the crib.

"What? Who, what?" He lunged up in a daze. "Is Elliot okay? Is he okay? Oh, my head."

"He looks fine," said Raj. "Been crying for a while. Can I feed him a bottle?"

Farb popped some pills. "I'll take care of it. Thanks for waking me up, guys." Farb mixed a bottle, shook it and popped it in Elliot's mouth. The baby drank like he'd spent weeks in the desert. "How long was he crying?"

"Few minutes. We heard it from the conference rooms. Guess he was really hungry."

Farb sat at his desk cradling the baby in one arm, and to the Nehrus' horror, continued to work with the other.

"Maybe you should take a rest?" suggested Rahul.

But Farb shook it off, even as his eyes blurred up and he dozed off again. The bottle fell out of Elliot's mouth and Farb startled himself awake as the baby began to cry.

"Please give us the baby Mr. Farb," said Rahul. "I'll feed him. Rest now. You must."

Farb had no fight left. He handed the baby to Rahul and let Raj lead him to the couch where a cold compress soothed him to sleep.

"Poor guy," Rahul said, and fed Elliot the bottle.

Raj wandered over to Farb's desk and couldn't help himself–he peeked at the pile of documents. "Ha! Production budgets? All this time Mr. Farb's been crunching the numbers for production budgets! Doesn't he know who I am? The king of production budgets. The Ferris Bueller of production budgets."

"Whoa, whoa. You're the Cameron of show budgets, I'm Bueller."

"That was never proven. It was a tie!"

"Oh please, the whole dorm room saw me win," said Raj.

"You cheated. You took performance enhancing drugs."

"Caffeine pills are not illegal. We never made that stipulation."

Elliot began to snore in Rahul's arms so he softly laid the baby in his crib next to George Carlin. "Let's settle this once and for all. First to finish is Ferris forever."

"You're on."

"No cheating this time."

The two brothers scrambled behind Farb's desk, elbowing each other for room as each dug into a massive pile. Five hours later, as morning sun leaked into the office, The Brothers were still at it. Farb was asleep, the baby snoring, until....

"I did it! I'm Ferris Bueller! And you're Principal Rooney!"

"I hate you! I hate you!" Rahul slammed down his pen.

"I told you! No one has ever beaten me. I'm like Judd Nelson and you're Molly Ringwald with lipstick in her cleavage."

Farb groaned awake, head pounding. When he managed to clear his eyes what he saw was Rahul Nehru giving his brother an old school wedgie. "What are you guys still doing here?" Farb croaked.

"Oh! Sorry Mr. Farb," Raj said, grabbing hold of his brother's flabby belly and pinching. "My brother's a sore loser."

"That's cheating!" Rahul released his brother's boxer shorts and patted himself down. "I hope you don't mind Mr. Farb. We've been competing for years over who can do production budgets faster."

"I always win," Raj said triumphantly.

"Do not!"

The wedgies recommenced and Farb scratched his head and walked over to the desk. There he saw two neat piles with budget numbers worked out from pre-production all the way to color correction on *Canadian Eye*–pilot, then options of six, thirteen and twenty-six episodes.

"Wait," said Farb, baffled. "You guys opened my work on the shows? You worked on this without even asking me?"

"I told you he'd be pissed," Raj muttered.

"We weren't thinking–it was late. We can undo it all today. Sorry Mr. Farb, we just got carried away."

"No, no," Farb said, leafing through the files in amazement. "You did all this work, just tonight?"

"Yes, sorry."

"Please don't fire us."

"Fire you?" Farb said. "Can you do more?"

Rahul elbowed his brother. "Double or nothing, Raj?"

"Call me Ferris."

10. TEAMWORK

The next several nights the Nehrus came by the office for their night shift with mushroom pizza and a six-pack of Dr. Pepper. If Farb was napping then one of the Brothers tended to Elliot and the other would work. If Elliot was asleep then it was all hands on deck. A pot of coffee was always on brew and, against his better judgment, Farb was smoking a few cigarettes just to stay alert. They stayed at it until past dawn most nights and though Farb was forced to nap more and more frequently, Rahul and Raj worked at a steady pace. The team's sole interruption came from Sid, the octogenarian security guard, who insisted they all salute him as if he was a four-star General. And of course there was Alicia Gordon. As if paid to distract them she had begun wearing outrageously skimpy outfits–tight see-through T-shirts, micro-minis and cherry red lipstick. She bust into Farb's office whenever she felt like it. "I'm bored. Strip poker anyone?"

The Nehrus were innocents: "No thanks, we're actualizing production budgets!"

Alicia rolled her eyes, call them "douches" and went back to Vapey.

Farb checked in with Shanna often. He tried to keep it light, assuring her that Elliot was just fine, and doing his best to let on that he wasn't done proving his point about the ease of parenting. But it was getting more difficult to explain why he so badly wanted Elliot by his side.

"He's mine too," Shanna would say. "And eventually we're going to have to spend time as a family."

"Real busy right now. And since you seem to have such a hard time with childcare on your own...."

"I never said that, Asshole. I just need some help."

"You got it," said Farb. "Elliot's happy here. I've got everything set up and he's sleeping well. So just enjoy the freedom."

"It's been a week since we've even sat down to talk, Jonathan. I don't like sleeping alone."

"Then don't."

Sometimes when they talked, Farb heard strange noises in the background, and though Shanna claimed it was just the TV, he could hear distant cars or even a man's cough in the background. Farb blocked it out. He would deal with Toulouse soon enough. Would it be easy to rig his balls to a car battery? For now it was just as well Shanna was occupied and out of the way even if it was with another man. Farb was getting work done and spending quality time with Elliot. For the moment his primary goals were fulfilled.

After one particularly long and productive all-nighter The Brothers convinced Farb it was time to get some real breakfast and fresh air. It would be good for the baby and for him. Farb popped three pills and tended to Elliot before they left. With repetition he had gotten the whole change-and-feed process to an under two minute pit stop.

"He looks like Peter Boyle in *Young Frankenstein,*" Raj remarked about Farb.

"More like Frau Blucher," corrected Rahul. "Remember how the horse would always neigh when they said her name?"

"Comedy gold."

"I can hear you guys," said Farb. "I'm aware this is not my best day."

"You smell like Frau Blucher too."

Farb carried Elliot out the door and past the huge stack of documents for *Canadian Eye* and *The Apologist.* "I seriously can't thank you guys enough," Farb said, flushed with gratitude.

"Don't sweat it Mr. Farb. It's about time someone let us do some real work around here. It's like we're invisible."

"About that."

"We know all about it," Rahul said. "We weren't exactly picture perfect Excellence in Diversity candidates. Partially our fault–we never corrected them when they asked us how long we'd been in Canada."

"Yeah, we were like 'a while.' Ha!"

The three men (and a baby) smiled as they waited for the elevator. But the smiles disappeared swiftly when the doors opened and out came Kyle Hershorn and Wyatt Cowper III, the two biggest douchebags in the office, and very possibly the world.

"Well if it isn't the Loser's Club?" Hershorn said, and on cue Cowper popped an L sign on his forehead.

"Morning Gentlemen," said Farb. "Done cruising middle schools and decided to come to work?"

"Very funny, Farb. The judge ruled it consensual for your information–and they were eighteen," said Hershorn.

"Old enough to be seven, old enough to be ate," snorted Cowper.

Hershorn shot him a look. "Anyways Farb–it's kind of pathetic watching you get all worked up over that *Apologist* dog."

"It's like an exercise in fatality," said Cowper.

"Futility, you idiot," Hershorn rolled his eyes. "Look I already told you Larson wants that pitch dead. Says it's worthless to everyone. So why kill yourself over it?"

"Because it's going to be a hit!" Rahul shot back.

"Ha! Wow, you've got some real attack dogs, Farb. The Excellence in Retardation crew."

"Can we tell him about the bet?" Cowper nudged Hershorn.

"Office pool," explained Hershorn. "Odds are three hundred to one your show goes to shit. You're screwed Farb."

"Put me down for a hundred that it makes it!" barked Raj.

"Wow! You've really got these idiots brainwashed Farb, and all because you carry around a baby. Believe me Mahatmas, when your photos came out, Farb was the first to call for your demotion."

"At least he doesn't fuck little boys," said Raj.

"They were little girls!" Cowper lunged at him.

Hershorn held him back. "Careful," he said to the Nehrus. "I may not be able to fire you, but I can make your lives a living hell, believe me." Hershorn turned to Farb. "Look at you Farb, Jesus Christ! You used to be okay–dressed slick, saunas at the Cambridge Club. You were almost cool for a married guy. Now you're a mess, you stink, and all for some idiotic idea that's going to probably get you fired. Why? Think you're going to start an early trust fund for the kid?" Hershorn went to stroke Elliot's head but Farb batted his hand away.

"Don't," he said seriously.

Hershorn backed off.

"Give it up," said Cowper. "Your just wasting company time. And after Monday's meeting you'll be back to stuttering your way through presentations for *Canadian Eye For The American Guy*."

Hershorn and Cowper strutted off, with Cowper giving the Brothers a sarcastic two thumbs up. Rahul and Raj replied with middle fingers.

"Nazis!" said Raj. "Full SS!"

Color drained from Farb's face as they entered the elevator–he lost balance. "Maybe we should skip brunch, guys," he said, teetering against the wall.

Raj quickly unstrapped Elliot, and Rahul held Farb up as they got him off the elevator and into the parking lot. "I'll drive, Mr. Farb. You're a mess."

They loaded Farb into the passenger's seat of his car and strapped Elliot in. "Everything's going to be okay. I'll follow close behind," said Raj.

Farb laid a newspaper over his face to block out the harsh morning sun as Rahul drove his Camry out into morning traffic. "You're going to be okay Mr. Farb—we'll get you home."

"Hershorn's right, you know," Farb said. "I'm just kidding myself about the *Apologist*. And I've dragged you two in as well. Shit, I've dragged Elliot in too...."

"Elliot's happy Mr. Farb. And don't worry about us. It's an adventure. Uh, will Mrs. Farb be home when we get there?"

"Depends if she's off fucking the obstetrician."

"Oh."

"I don't know where things went so wrong, Raj," Farb continued. "I had a plan at some point and it seemed even to be working, but everything's chaos now. My marriage is non-existent, my career in shambles. And now I'm left with no time and the feeling that I've totally wasted my life. Take my advice Rahul and get out of TV—it's a shit career choice."

Rahul looked over at Farb with his newspaper on his face—he wasn't sure he'd ever seen anything so depressing, but he knew he had to take Farb's mind off things. Somehow, that was his job. "We all have regrets," he began. "Like me and Raj. We got this stupid job that's beneath us and instead of quitting we've just been riding it acting like we won the Lotto 6/49. We get paid and do what we want but really we're just playing more videogames and watching more Netflix, which is cool but it's like we're still teenagers. You know, Hershorn's right about us being losers. I mean I wouldn't want to put us in a corporate newsletter either. Not to mention the last time I had a girlfriend was high school. Sometimes I think the best thing me and my brother could do is to split up. We're so co-dependant, I mean, we share everything: books, clothes, a bunk bed. It's madness."

Elliot giggled from the backseat.

"Wait, heh-heh. You guys sleep in a bunk bed?" Farb couldn't help it either and snorted laughter through the newspaper.

"We have a small apartment!" Rahul said, suddenly defensive.

Farb and Elliot burst out laughing in unison. "But a bunk bed! Ha-ha!"

"So your wife's cheating on you with the baby doctor and I'm the laughingstock?"

"Kinda."

"No, you're right," Rahul shook his head. "Two grown men in a bunk bed. Jesus."

At home, Farb found a note from Shanna saying she was out running errands. All the better—no need to deal with her in his state. There was too much to explain, too much subtext that he didn't have the energy for. What Farb really needed was sleep, but with Elliot wide awake after napping in the car, he decided to give the boy a bath instead. There was a big day ahead based on The List, a major milestone, so Farb wanted Elliot clean and in a fresh outfit before they got going.

Incidentally, bathing Elliot was the one parenting task that didn't cause Farb panic. The baby's fearlessness in the tub was a special point of pride for him; he heard that most kids Elliot's age were terrified of the water and that helpless parents had to wash them down with wet cloths in the sink. Not Elliot—the kid was a champ. Farb filled the tub up to his belly and Elliot just giggled and thrashed around in delight. Today, as a special gift for good behavior, Farb introduced his son to bubble bath. He eased it under the warm tap until the bubbles spread all around. Elliot observed the bubbles very seriously, then with an expression of total glee went crazy for them and splashed around. "Those are bubbles! Bubbles!" Farb exclaimed. One of the privileges of parenthood is watching your child discover something miraculous that adults take for granted.

–Forces you to reconsider the mundane: "Let me get this straight" the baby was basically saying, "these are floating air pockets with little rainbows inside that also have the power to clean? Oh my God." Farb wondered if he had retained any ability to consider nature's mysteries with the awe they deserved. He might yawn at a unicorn. "Little floating air pockets, with rainbows inside, shiny, floating air bubbles." Farb concentrated. He was onto something too, the incoming tide of epiphany perhaps, when, instead of experiencing a flash of enlightenment, Farb experienced a violent stabbing to his temples that knocked him right off the toilet seat and onto the bathroom floor. Sharp pain like nails in his skull, then a torrent of nails, a hailstorm of electric nails that filled his vision with red dots and green squares until everything was pulsating red-blackness. "WHOA!" Farb dug into his pocket but couldn't find his pills–his vision failed completely and Farb thrashed into the tub to get hold of Elliot so that he didn't fall face first into the water. Elliot cried out as his body met the cold air and water splashed onto the floor. "It's okay baby, okay little boy. You're okay, you're okay." Elliot struggled, desperate to be back with his precious bubbles, but Farb gripped tighter as he crawled along the soaked bathroom floor. A lightning storm ignited in his brain. "WHERE ARE THOSE FUCKING PILLS?!" Crawling out into the hall, hitting the sharp corners of doors with his shoulders, shielding Elliot, the baby struggled harder and Farb squeezed tighter and the crying turned to terrified screeches. When Farb reached his bedroom, he lay Elliot on the carpet and searched blindly for his briefcase and pried it open on the bed. Documents and pens flew everywhere and he worried that Elliot might get a hold of something sharp, when finally he found the pills and shoved them into his mouth. Farb fell back onto the floor, found Elliot, wrapped him tightly in a blanket and bounced him in his arms as fast as he could to ease

the panic. "It's okay—Daddy's here baby—shush-shush-shushhhhh."
Elliot couldn't be consoled and relief took forever, the drugs getting comfortable, being lazy until finally, finally the red-black
spots that darkened his world turned yellow and green and finally
brushed away from his eyeballs like clumps of dirt over a coffin.
He saw again, but it was even worse than blindness: the look of
fear and distrust on Elliot's face broke Farb down to tears himself.
He'd put Elliot in danger. The one person that mattered to him,
and it killed him a thousand times. "I'm sorry, baby. I'm so sorry."
Farb wasn't capable of caring for Elliot anymore. He couldn't even
protect himself.

Farb found a pacifier and carried the baby back to his room to
get changed. Despite narrowly escaping disaster, there was business to get done and no stopping now. On the dresser was a gag
gift from one of his McGill buddies—a three-piece pinstripe onesie
replete with a red silk kerchief. A still-attached note read: "He's
almost ready for Bay Street. Now just teach him to bullshit." Farb
smiled as he zipped up the outfit and added the little socks that
were knit to look like Oxford shoes. Perfection.

Farb wrote a note to Shanna saying that he would be home
in a few hours, then loaded the baby back into the car. It was still
a monumental day in Elliot's life and he couldn't be late. Farb
fished a yarmulke out of the glove compartment, popped two more
pills, and pulled out of the driveway in a hurry.

The congregation at Temple Beth-El was small for such an event,
there weren't even enough men for a minion but Rabbi Klotz agreed
to do it anyway. In addition to Farb, Elliot and the Rabbi, there
was George the janitor, Cantor Rosen with her acoustic guitar, and
Ethel Posner—an elderly lady, mostly deaf—who came to all events.
Farb's stricken demeanor worried the Rabbi. He might need medical attention or faint mid-service, the Rabbi thought. Farb's skin

was pale and clammy, and with his suit still damp from the bathtub debacle he appeared almost mad. But he beamed with pride as he held Elliot next to the *bema*. The Rabbi read over his notes then faced the congregation with his trademark endearing smile. "For the *Sh'ma,* please turn to page six-hundred and thirty-nine."

Coming to this moment had not been easy for Farb and certainly wasn't cheap. When he first presented the idea to Rabbi Klotz his response was immediate.

"Absolutely not," he had said, looking at Farb like he was a lunatic.

"But why?"

"Why?" the Rabbi squinted. "Why?! Because the Torah says so. Specifically that a boy is not to be Bar Mitzvahed until his thirteenth year. It's *Halacha,* Jewish Law, God's words. Plus, how could a baby read from the Torah? I'm sorry, I know you must have your reasons but my answer is a firm and final no."

"It would mean a great deal to me Rabbi," Farb said, insistent, then slid a check made out to the Rabbi's Sabbatical Fund across his desk. "A great deal."

The Rabbi eyed the figure written on the check and his face froze seemingly forever as his life passed before him—from idealistic rabbinical student, to earnest neophyte Assistant Rabbi, to jaded Rabbi insecure about his contract renewal and jeopardized by his inability to attract charitable donations.

"With the Torah there are so many interpretations," the Rabbi said, a tentative smile spreading across his face. "Who's to say really who can and cannot be a man in the eyes of The Almighty."

After Cantor Rosen sang a few prayers, melodiously finger picking her guitar, the Rabbi delivered a short but effective sermon citing an obscure passage from the Talmud to substantiate Elliot's early Bar Mitzvah. "Adonai himself proclaimed that it is the age of the spirit not the body that allows a man to be measured in the eyes of God! In the case of Elliot Ben-Joshua Farb the soul is at least thirteen more likely fourteen years old."

"Amen!" George the janitor cried out extra loud as he pressed the button to reveal the Torah.

"What's that you said?" Ethel Posner asked loudly.

"Amen!" George repeated.

"Oh, right. Well let's get on with this shindig."

The Rabbi motioned for Farb to step forward. Farb stepped to the podium, passed Elliot into the Rabbi's arms, then unfolded his speech. He looked at Elliot who (although asleep and in a gag onesie) he imagined to be a fully pubescent thirteen year old—with braces, teen acne and a lanky athletic build. It was easy now. Thirteen year-old Elliot was in a blue pinstripe suit with shined shoes (but also white gym socks in a stubborn display of adolescent independence) and appeared ready to step into manhood. Farb looked out to the rows of empty seats and imagined a large crowd of family members there, business associates and (unfortunately) Shanna and Greenblatt sitting side by side. He felt the fear of addressing the crowd and stepped into it this time.

"You know, a lot of people think that a thirteen year-old boy is nothing more than a pimply sarcasm-machine with a mouth full of orthodontia and a web-porn addiction. And while the truth may be on their side, the Torah tells a different story."

"Amen to that," Ethel Posner called out. "Preach brother, preach!"

"Under Jewish law, once a boy is Bar Mitzvahed he has certain responsibilities—he is eligible to read from the Torah, can participate in a minion—can even marry. He is no longer an innocent. Traditionally the parents of the Bar Mitzvah give thanks to God that they no longer have to carry the burden of their child's sins. And on this day of my son Elliot's Bar Mitzvah to that I say a resounding Amen."

"Amen!" George called out.

"Amen!" cried Ethel.

"For example, just this summer I received an eight-hundred dollar phone bill with a long list of mysterious phone numbers cited. After a thorough investigation and a call to my old basketball buddy Don Iveson who just happens to be a VP at Bell Canada, the calls were traced back to a phone booth in Orillia, Ontario where my son attends Jewish summer camp. Turns out Elliot shared my calling card number with fellow camper, Allison Bloom, a fourteen year-old blonde of loose morals who I have since learned provided Elliot with his first sexual experience. Allison then disseminated the calling card number as freely as she seems to disseminate her favors, and soon half the camp was calling home on my dime, the other half presumably engaged more directly with Allison herself. The investigation managed to cull *some* of the stolen funds, but I was forced to pay the outstanding bill of three-eighty, not exactly bargain basement for your son to get his first hand job."

"Amen again," Ethel Posner muttered, then fell asleep.

"But Elliot must not be judged for his maturity or lack thereof. He's a good kid, hard working and curious, and at six-foot-one with size thirteen feet, the old adage 'act your age not your shoe size' does not apply. There was a time I feared Elliot might grow freakishly tall and require expensive custom-made clothes. I took him to a specialist who x-rayed his wrist and measured his testicles against a series of wooden balls tied together on a chain. The balls varied in size from a pea to a cantaloupe and were numbered and lettered. I am proud to announce on this day that Elliot is packing an impressive G-24. Not quite Elephantiasis, but fully ripened and healthy. Oh yeah, he'll be six-three at full growth." Farb scanned the crowd and located visions of Shanna and Greenblatt. Two rows behind them he imagined his own new companion, a leggy blonde with the Canadian Olympic Swim Team. "I would like to take this opportunity to thank Temple Beth-El for the lovely service. Rabbi Klotz, your sermon on the ills of intermarriage was eloquent and well-informed. I would have appreciated it if you hadn't stared directly at my lovely blonde companion, Christy, while proclaiming: 'Let us not give Hitler a victory!' but I admire your passion. You've come a long way since your moralistic critique of Israel's bombing of Iraq's nuclear plant. It was a lapse into *faux*-liberal defeatism and I acknowledge your written apology in last year's *B'sherit Newsletter.* I mean, can you imagine if the Iraqis had full nuclear capabilities when they invaded Kuwait? The Free World should be kissing Israeli ass!"

"That is not to say we are above criticism at home. Membership here at Temple Beth-El costs a pretty penny particularly for those who don't lie about their income bracket. No thanks to the success of my hit show *Canada's Next Great Apologist,* now in its twelfth season, the sliding scale membership fee does not exactly work in my favor. Yet upon seeing a list of members in each category, I would like to publicly call: bullshit. Izzie Morgenstein of Nesbitt, McMaster & Delacroix who made a killing in *Blue Torrent* (we're talking in the tens of millions) is in the 'Mid-Salary' category? Eli Rosenblatt of Rosenblatt & Rosenblatt is 'Low-Income'? In what galaxy! 'Look,' I told the membership committee, 'I'll pay the average. I won't lie like the others but I also won't be robbed! I will pay the average.'"

"Speaking of deception, my ex-wife Shanna is here today with her new impossibly *meeskite* husband whom I can only refer to as 'Toulouse Lautrec.' My wife began her tryst with the dwarf right here in this very synagogue at choir practice. I figured I was safe since only dandies do choir, but I did not account for a reprobate obstetrician. Toulouse and Shanna first met professionally when he helped deliver my son Elliot at Toronto General, and it turns out that while Elliot wanted out of Shanna's womb that day, Toulouse wanted in. Is there a better candidate to be struck by lightning? I ask!"

"Look, no one argues that divorce is a good thing—it takes its toll particularly on the children and I worry about its effect on Elliot. For a boy on the cusp of manhood to be abandoned by his mother can do irreparable harm. Recently Elliot has exhibited moments of melancholy, there has been trouble at school, calls from the principal, poor math scores, and, if the amount of time he spends locked in the bathroom is any indication, chronic masturbation has also been a side effect. But strong genes have kept him resilient. Elliot attends Upper Canada College, an esteemed private school with a tough admissions exam and interview process. He fought me on it—UCC's strict blazer dress code and their 'boys-only' rule were both reasons he resisted. But I reasoned with him—it's import-ant to learn to be around a cross-section of people, particularly the Wasps, who last time I checked still run this town. Plus I bought him an electric guitar."

"In closing, I wish you all a lovely time at this evening's festivities. Enjoy the buffet. In Jewish Law, if the Torah is dropped while it is carried to the Arc, the congregation must fast for forty days. That's a long time to go without Doritos. And though several of the attendees could certainly benefit from such a diet plan, I'm glad it was avoided—the *ruggelach* alone cost $14.39 a pound and it would be a shame to put it to waste."

"Elliot, on this monumental day my cup overfloweth. You're a good kid and I'm confident that you will blossom into manhood with grace and swagger. Still what's the big rush? These halcyon days of youth will soon fade, and, before you know it, innocent schoolboy crushes will turn to marriage, which, if you have the misfortune of marrying a black belt in deception, will become a failed marriage. My deepest hope is that you avoid such bitter betrayal in your lifetime and find only happiness and loyalty. Also, my deepest hope is that Toulouse has a fatal seizure during the *Hava Negilah,* but this is not an appropriate time to dwell on personal matters. *L'Chaim* and *Mazel Tov* to the Bar Mitzvah Boy!"

11. THE CUCKQUEAN

Since her run-in with Shanna Farb at the grocery store, Carol Greenblatt was a mess. She prayed it was just paranoia, her imagination getting the best of her, but women's intuition informed her that the little swan with the long black curls and arched ass was secretly fucking her husband. She could smell it on her–youth mixed with age and, yes, marijuana and horseshit. The thought made her ill. Carol retrieved the prescription bottle that Raymond picked up for her and worked the child safety lid. Her hands shook so much that when she finally got it open the bottle flew from her hands and scattered pills all over the floor. Down on her hands and knees, Carol located each pill and removed bits of carpet fabric that clung to them. She needed new carpeting, that was for sure. As much as she vacuumed and conditioned, the poor quality of the fabric caused shedding! Re-carpeting would be costly, choosing a new carpet could take her months. But as she detached little bits of lint off the pills, she also noticed something peculiar about their texture. They were smoother than usual, more rounded at the edges, and she wondered if the manufacturer had changed the design to make them easier to swallow. She cleaned off two pills and swallowed them, also noticing a pleasant new fruity flavor. Oh everyone was upgrading–even anxiety medication had to taste like candy. She could at least buy newly woven carpets! Carol grabbed the phone, deciding to just flat out confront Raymond about this Shanna Farb girl, but of course he didn't pick up. She tried the hospital's main line and was told he hadn't checked in but that they had him listed as on-call. "Well that's too peculiar," Carol said. "He wouldn't reschedule without telling me."

For five years Ray was always on-call the same day. Why would he switch it now? Carol sat on the edge of the bed calming herself, but the unsolved puzzle pieces plagued her. Raymond had been on-call only last week. If this had something to do with this Farb girl, she wanted to know now and, though the thought of getting back in the car gave her cold chills, she decided that it had to be done or she would have a full on anxiety attack. So Carol forced herself out of the house without even checking the messages, even ignoring her strong suspicion that the oven had a slow gas leak that would surely blow the house to smithereens. She drove by the hospital first but only had to pass the parking lot to see that Raymond's spot was empty. She looped past Raymond's hang-outs–the YMCA, the Second Cup at York Mills and Leslie, the Soft Serve at Bayview Village. But who was she kidding playing spy? Raymond could be anywhere, on Queen Street visiting that antique dealer or even back home waiting for her with a logical explanation for everything! Carol decided on one last stop before heading home, and drove the tree-lined streets towards Temple Beth-El. "Either I'll make a fool of myself or I'll avoid a lot of trouble!" she said, glancing into the rear view mirror horrified that she wasn't wearing any makeup.

There were a handful of cars in the synagogue's parking lot and she didn't recognize any other than the Rabbi's blue Pontiac. She walked to the synagogue's main doors not even sure what she was doing there and found that they opened easily (not broken in the slightest despite what her husband told her). Inside Carol heard Cantor Rosen's unmistakable soprano-and-acoustic-guitar combo echoing down the hall. Maybe there was a service? She hadn't noticed anything in the events calendar. Maybe the choir was in there right now performing–that would explain Raymond's whereabouts. It also gave her pause. She was in sweatpants with no makeup spying on her husband–she would look like a fool. Raymond never wanted her around too much in public and the way she was put together now, well no one would be too shocked if he did abandon his wife of twenty-two years for some young thing! She ducked into the bathroom to touch up.

"What a mess Carol. Sweatpants, really?" She eyed herself in the mirror–the thin red varicose veins showing themselves on her plump cheeks, her mousy lifeless hair, the neck wrinkled like a rhinoceros. It hadn't bothered her this much before. "Time to get back on the hobby horse Carol, no more snacks!" The thought of Shanna Farb with her long graceful neck and firm upper arms burned her up.

Adequately touched up, Carol walked the warm carpeted halls of Beth-El. She reached the main sanctuary and put her ear to the door. She heard the Rabbi's voice and then another male voice take over. The man seemed to be delivering a speech and was especially energized. Carol couldn't help her curiosity. She creaked the wooden door just a sliver. What she saw inside was more perplexing than she could have imagined. There seemed to be a midget in a three-piece suit being prayed over by the Rabbi. A man with dark hair and a long sickly face stood at the *bema* ranting about his ex-wife while an elderly lady slept open-mouthed in the front row. Carol stepped back from the door utterly baffled. She shuffled quickly down the hall toward the exit, trying to shake it off and figured she must be going insane. Surely, this whole foray was a deeply embarrassing mistake and she should go home immediately. Raymond was probably already there wondering where she was. His questioning might even put her on the defensive and empower Raymond to lie to her about the woman with the black curly hair, if there was anything to lie about at all.

Carol exited from the same door in which she had come in but darted behind a pillar when she heard voices headed her way. No need to have an awkward run-in, especially the way she was dressed. She turned a corner and sidled along the synagogue, stepping lightly on wet grass and crusty mud. Just out of curiosity, she followed the wall to the side window and indeed there was an orange cone there–the basement window was held open precariously, obviously used for entry and there were some remnants of mud and manure at the base. So Raymond *was* telling the truth! Oh, it was definitely time to go–maybe cook Raymond a brisket for dinner, and then... CRACK! Down in the steep fall of the ravine below Carol heard the crack of branches followed by a series of high-pitched giggles. The giggle was familiar and it was followed by more cracks and the sound of rustling leaves. Carol sniffed the air deeply and detected the vaguest scent of her husband. "Raymond is that you? Ray?" So he was lying. She would catch the bastard with his pants around his ankles after all! The leaves on the hill were slick and who knew what lived down there but as the giggling grew louder, Carol took her first step down and found the ground solid enough. She held on to trunks of maple trees and edged her way down to where a narrow walking trail led to flat ground. Already her sneakers were muddied but she was happy she'd wore them if only to provide the alibi of a brisk nature walk if she got caught snooping. She walked more briskly and moved her arms aerobically to fool possible onlookers. But when she heard the giggle again the façade went right out the window–she ducked and scrambled out of sight with the adeptness and precision of a sniper, then darted from tree to tree fifty yards across the ravine, following a thin scent-trail of weed. Her nose never lied. It was really happening, and when she spotted smoke wafting in the air behind a fallen log she knew she had him–that son of a bitch!

"I KNEW IT! I JUST KNEW IT!" Carol jumped several feet in the air to the other side of the tree trunk and appeared flat-footed before the two lovers like some deranged boar. "I CAUGHT YOU! CAUGHT YOU RED HANDED, YOU RED-FACED COCKSUCKER!"

"Holy Crap."

But it wasn't Raymond at all. It was a couple of skinny stoned teenagers with long hair and hooded sweatshirts passing an apple bong between them.

"You're not Raymond," Carol accused the startled kids. "Oh my God, aren't you...."

"Mrs. Greenblatt? What are you doing down here?"

It was Taryn Rabinowitz, her daughter Beth's friend from tennis camp. Carol thought fast and assumed her best school principal voice. "Well, I should be asking you the same thing, young lady? I don't suppose you're studying for finals?"

The young girl blushed but her boyfriend, more brash or possibly more high said, "We're smoking an apple bong–looks like you could use a hit?"

"Lowell shut up!" Taryn smacked her boyfriend who just cracked up more. "Please don't tell my mom about this Mrs. Greenblatt? She thinks I'm like, perfect or something."

"Yeah, she'll take away your Jeep Cherokee," the boy laughed.

"You drive it too, asshole!"

They squabbled more and Taryn kept slapping her boyfriend on the head. Great, Carol thought, these two will make a perfect married couple someday.

"Why don't we let this be our little secret?" Carol forced a smile. "But you should really think of choosing better company if you want to go somewhere in life. This one seems rude, Taryn."

"Okay Mrs. Greenblatt. Thanks. I'll think about that."

"Yeah thanks lady. Cool advice."

Taryn smacked her boyfriend again until they both started laughing. Carol chuckled to herself too–had the second hand smoke hit her? I must be going nuts.

Carol climbed back up the trail, damning herself for being so silly, for dreaming up a scenario in which her husband would betray her so brazenly when she heard voices from above in the synagogue parking lot. Just great! The service has been let out! Now she'd have to wait there hidden in the ravine until all the cars were gone! She ducked behind a tree and sat on a wet stump just far enough away that she would go unnoticed and avoid another potential sighting. And that's when she saw them. Up almost directly above her by a parked car. Raymond and that skinny bitch from the grocery store. She blinked herself out of possible hysteria, but there they were–kissing, hugging, and then, before Carol could force herself off the stump and perhaps commit double homicide, jumping into a car and driving off. Carol lost her footing and her knee plunged into a moist pile of muck. "SON OF A BITCH!" she yowled. "No wonder he didn't want me at choir practice." Then a sickly rush of acid soured her stomach as it dawned on her: Raymond had never been able to keep her away from anything before. Even her therapist said no one could stop Carol but Carol. Yet somehow she'd cooped herself up rather than join the choir as she'd planned to and thereby allowed her husband to cheat freely? Inconceivable! Carol flung her purse on the ground and ripped open the bottle of pills that Raymond had picked up for her at Shopper's Drugmart. The prescription written on the bottle was just as always but when she emptied the pills into her hand she saw it again–the slightly smoothed ridge, the edges rounded more than the pills she'd been popping for almost two years. Switched! Carol emptied the bottle into the mud and let out a bestial roar that echoed through the ravine. "FUUUUCK–AAARRGH!"

"Are you okay Mrs. Greenblatt?" Taryn called up.

"Oh yes dear," Carol coughed. "Just swallowed wrong is all."

Carol stomped up the rest of the ravine, branches scratching her arms but she didn't give a rat's ass. Her mind was busy decoding the icy elaborateness of her husband's betrayal–the sinister nature of it. Swapping medication? Didn't he take an oath?! She winced at what an easy target she'd been for him, how predictable she'd become–not a speeding ticket in twenty years, not a dentist visit missed or an episode of 60 Minutes unwatched. A dependably boring person. All the time writing an instruction manual for her husband to deceive her, training for Cuckquean Of The Year! As Carol reached her car, another thought burned in her mind. The sex. She'd chalked Raymond's more selfish sexual proclivities up to a mid-life crisis, the adolescent patch he seemed to be trapped in. Carol had acquiesced too–marriage is long, there are so many lives, and if that's what he needed to get the through the loneliness of having the girls off at university then she would humor him for a bit–just like the marijuana, the man-cave, and the beard. But now–now–she saw that it was not that at all. He wanted blowjobs so that he could imagine someone else doing it! "I'll cut his nuts clear off his body!"

Carol's car screeched out of the parking lot and raced through a bevy of stop signs on the way back to the house. "Raaaaymond! Where are you?" She ripped open the front door and left the keys hanging there. "I want to see your disgraceful face now!" But the house was cold and dark. She thought she heard a creak in the basement so she stomped past the kitchen to the door leading to Raymond's man cave and banged.

"Raymond? Don't you hide from me."

No response. Carol had not ventured down into the basement in ages. There could have been a pot farm down there for all she knew. It was the one concession she'd submitted to from couples' therapy. Raymond needed a place of his own where he wouldn't be disturbed, and though she would rather have had the basement re-finished so that the girls could have another option to stay at the house on their visits, she gave over control and even arranged for a housekeeper to tidy up down there once in a while. But the rules were off now obviously. "Raymond did you hear me? I'm calling you!"

It was cold and fusty and the stairs creaked as Carol stepped down. She flipped on the light switch and a single naked bulb illuminated over a plain gray working table. A small bookshelf and a rusty toolbox were set in the corner. Ugh. More like a torture chamber than an office. The small windows were covered with black fabric. This is where he likes to unwind? –Figures–she married a sadist. Carol poked around hoping to find some evidence of Ray's deceit. First thing she tried was the desk drawer, locked, but a small key was taped predictably to the bottom of the drawer. Inside she found a stack of manuals for antique weaponry and then a red velvet case, inside of which she found a gun. It was old and military-style, but a gun nonetheless! Her pulse quickened as she picked it up, surprised at the weight. "That idiot! To bring a gun into the house with children around. So irresponsible!" She held it up to the naked bulb and saw bullets in there. Carol tried picking them out with her fingernails but stopped when out the tiny rectangular window she heard her husband's distant voice. "Thanks Fred–I'll get these back to you for the weekend."

Carol moved quickly. She tiptoed her way up the stairs worried like hell the floorboards would crack and she would shoot herself in the head. She made it to the kitchen just as keys jingled at the front door and sat as Greenblatt stepped into the house. "Carol? You left the keys in the door again," Greenblatt called out. "Sweetie?"

A flush of cowardice overtook Carol and she tucked the gun into her sweatshirt. Maybe it was better she didn't confront him after all? Maybe this would all go away; it was just something in marriage, perhaps in all marriages, something they could solve in therapy. Surely she hadn't been herself since the girls left and maybe she'd pushed him away? Carol's mouth dried to cotton and what she feared most was that her voice would crack, revealing her as weak and scared just when she needed to be strong. Carol squeezed the handle of the pistol and that gave her assurance. Yes, she had his balls right in the palm of her hand! Raymond could say anything he wanted now. She had the power. He could suck *her* dick.

Greenblatt entered the kitchen, casually tossing his jacket on the counter and Carol tightened her grip on the gun. She'd worked hard to clear a space for his coats in the hall closet, but look how little he cared!

"Hey honey. I was just next door borrowing some plaster. I think the window frames are cracked in the foyer."

"Sit down, please, Raymond," she said.

"Nah, I think I'm going to head downstairs and relax. Crazy day at the hospital. Two sets of twins, respiratory problems. Just go ahead and eat without me, I'll heat something up." Greenblatt pulled open the basement door and Carol knew it was now or never.

"You weren't at the hospital Ray."

"Sure I was," Greenblatt said. "New system. They're totally disorganized in reception. I'm on level three, North Wing. Wasn't my cell on?"

"STOP LYING!" Carol screamed. She banged the table with her palm—a coffee mug jumped—and Greenblatt froze in his tracks.

"Did you take your medication today, Honey?" Greenblatt asked cautiously.

"I saw you with her Raymond. In the parking lot at Temple Beth-El. I saw you and her. Kissing!"

"I'm, uh, not sure what you're talking about, Carol. Kissing who?"

"Her! Her! You son of a bitch!" Carol steadied herself, remembering the gun, the gun, the gun....

Greenblatt patted a glaze of sweat on his forehead. "It's-it's not the way you saw. It's far more complicated. She's a patient."

Carol held back tears. She wanted him to struggle, choke on his bullshit. But nothing could prepare her for how Raymond finally responded to her accusation of adultery. He could have denied it or cried or fallen to his knees and pleaded for forgiveness, or better yet confronted her for her sins in their marriage, and then they could have fought it out. It might get messy, but they could fight it out and stay together–at least that would be something real. Instead Greenblatt chuckled. It was a smirk at first, possibly a nervous one from the relief that comes with being caught in a lie, but then his face split into a devilish chuckle that Carol recognized from years of interpreting his stupid face as representing only one emotion in her husband: Pride. He was fucking proud of himself and couldn't hold it in!

"You saw her?" Greenblatt said, almost giggling. "I mean us, you saw us?"

"I caught you."

"Wow!" Greenblatt laughed outright and caught his hand over his mouth. He was ashamed of his reaction and saw it was hurtful to Carol, but he couldn't help himself. All this time with Shanna there was only one thing missing: a witness. Someone to see that he, Raymond Greenblatt "most likely to remain a nerd" in his High School, was in a consensual sexual relationship with a hot chick. And Jewish too! It was unfortunate it had to be Carol, but it had to be somebody! In a way Greenblatt thought she'd be proud of him. "She's twenty-eight years old," he beamed. "Does anyone else know? Is it public information?"

Carol's face contorted with disgust. Greenblatt read it as understanding. He took a step forward and extended a pleading gesture to his wife. Maybe she saw how important this was to him and would allow him to continue?

"I've fallen in love Carol. I can't fight that." And strengthened by this line of reasoning, as if the truth alone had some moral high ground he continued. "And eventually, eventually I am going marry her. For the first time in my life I'm really in love. Can't you be happy for me Carol?"

"You dare!?" Carol roared.

"I know how you must feel. And I'm so sorry, I really am. I've always cared for you. I haven't been perfect but I've tried as a husband. But I've never felt like this. I need to spread my wings. And I know you think it's all some stupid mid-life crisis but I know this is real."

Carol scratched the gun through her sweatshirt. Maybe she should just shoot him? Watch him bleed. He deserved it, that's for sure. But as she looked him over (with his stupid beard and his stoner's eyes) it was harder to see the malicious cheat that merited death than a pathetic boy being led by his boner. Through her sweatshirt Carol pointed the gun in his direction just to see if she could do it and it wasn't even a question–she could kill him with ease. But what would that do?

"You're a coward," Carol said matter of factly. "A coward and a child."

"Maybe," Greenblatt had the nerve to reply. "Or maybe this is the most courageous thing I've done in my life."

"Oh shut up you dickwad! Get out of my house and don't you think of coming back. You have my blessing Ray–go be with your little slut! Go be with her. Start a band, listen to the Grateful Dead, I don't care. Just don't speak!"

Carol grabbed the coffee mug off the table and hurled it. Greenblatt had no time to react except to cover his face. The cup shattered against the fridge.

"COWARD!"

Greenblatt removed his hands from his face and tiptoed out of the kitchen.

"Bye for now," he muttered, walking out, but then returned seconds later. "Uh, forgot my, uh, coat."

12. DISCOVERY

Elliot snored as Farb carried him up to his bedroom. The baby had a right to be tired–becoming a man under Jewish law was exhausting work, and he'd met the challenge with panache. Farb was the proudest Jewish Dad in Canada.

Shanna was sitting up in bed when he got home so Farb knew he was in for a confrontation. He'd done his best to avoid his wife over the past two weeks and had been surprisingly successful. Now he just had to hold her off for one more day, then it would be time to finally spill the beans. But not yet.

Farb laid Elliot into his crib and kissed him on the forehead. "You did good today," he whispered. "Sweet dreams, Big Man." He flipped on some Baby Einstein (because who knows?) and headed into the bedroom.

Shanna sat up reading a gossip magazine and did her best to avoid eye contact when Farb entered.

"Did he sleep long in the car?" she asked.

"Half hour. But don't worry, I ran him ragged with new adventures. He'll sleep right through the night."

Shanna wanted to know what new adventures Jonathan was talking about and why he was wearing a wrinkled suit and why the bathroom floor in Elliot's room was drenched, for that matter, but she focused on the larger issue. "We have to talk, Jonathan. The distance between us is not healthy."

"We'll be fine," Farb said and head into the bathroom. He turned on the shower extra hot and let the steam rise into his sinuses to ease his headache. Dr. Arupal's warnings had increased in seriousness lately, a new MRI revealed that the tumor was growing slightly. Procrastination, Arupal explained, was a veritable death sentence.

But Farb couldn't slow down. If he took even a moment to rest, his entire system would shut down, and with his big meeting in Montreal only hours away he couldn't risk it.

Farb wiped the fog from the mirror and took a long hard look at himself. His eyes were bloodshot, his hairline somehow receded by inches. His gut hadn't shrunk though—no justice in the world. "Hang in there big guy," he said aloud.

"Going somewhere?" Shanna called from the bedroom.

"Big pitch meeting in Montreal tomorrow early. Working late, then off to the airport. Why, planning some more leisure time?"

"Just wanted to know," Shanna sighed.

"If all goes well I'll be back in the afternoon. Then I'll take a few days off. We can talk then." Farb grabbed his bag and was heading out when Shanna said:

"I never wanted money. The other night you said you were trying to get money for me. But I never wanted money. I only want to be loved."

Farb bit down hard—this had to wait. "Just take care of Elliot, okay? He's a man now. A real man in God's eyes." Then Farb ran out to the car, holding his bag over his head to block the rain. He flipped on his windshield wipers but forgot the headlights, causing an oncoming car to swerve slightly as he passed.

Shanna sat up in bed unable to derive any joy from her gossip magazines. She didn't like Jonathan being so cryptic. What was "he's a man now in God's eyes" supposed to mean? Probably a slight against her mothering abilities. But then look at him. He looked like a zombie—pale and unshaven with dark circles under his eyes. It's exactly how she felt when she was left alone with the baby for days. Finally, her husband was getting a taste of how hard childrearing is—surely he was due for a crash just like she had after her first few months of sleep deprivation. And when he lost it Shanna would finally have her opportunity to gloat, to force Farb to admit that she worked hard too, that she was useful and should be respected as a full partner in their marriage and not a glorified maid. Finally she'd get some respect.

Shanna found Elliot sleeping soundly in his crib, though inexplicably wearing a three-piece suit onesie. But it was adorable! She felt a tinge of guilt noticing that Elliot was bigger, his black hair fuller. That she had missed even a moment of the baby's growth just to prove a point to her husband made her ill. She leaned down and kissed the baby's cheek, but before she could change him into pajamas she heard Jonathan's cell ring from the bedroom. Was he back? She didn't hear the door open. Shanna followed the ring into the bathroom where the mirrors were still fogged up. She found the it under a towel on the counter. "Hello? Hello?" She missed it, but the phone soon buzzed and the small screen read "New Message." Probably Jonathan trying to locate it. Shanna dialed 1.

"You have one new voice message," the automotive system said. "Yes, I am calling you again," a woman's voice said, annoyed. It was a familiar foreign voice that Shanna couldn't quite place until: "It's important you come in for treatment Mr. Farb—those pills can lose potency and become ineffective." It was Dr. Arupal. "You risk having seizures and possibly going into a coma if we don't begin immediately, okay? Look, many of our patients experience a kind of denial when they learn about a tumor but it's not an end—there are many advanced treatments. You could have years of happy living with your family by your side." Shanna dropped the phone as if electrocuted by it. She fell into a heap and let out a serious of wild shrieks. Everything flooded in—the long days, the odd behavior, the migraines, even the extra time with Elliot all fell into place. Jonathan was dying. Shanna dialed his office but there was only the message. She ran back into Elliot's room and carried him out of his crib. He was so tired his body fell slack and heavy against her chest. "It's okay, baby—Mommy's here. Mommy will protect you. Damn it, Jonathan, why couldn't you tell me?" She had to think. Who to call at the hospital? Who did she know who could help? How could she have been so blind!? The doorbell rang. Shanna flinched—it was after nine. Maybe something happened to Jonathan on the road? Maybe it was an ambulance or the police? The doorbell rang again several times and she ran down the stairs half expecting the entire fire department to bust in. Instead, standing there in the rain like a wet dog, was Greenblatt.

"She knows!" he exclaimed joyfully. Greenblatt lunged forward and kissed Shanna, pressing himself against the baby. "Carol knows! She saw us together. And I told her. I told her that I love you and that I want to be with you!" His eyes were wild and red like some madman off his meds. Shanna looked nervously out into the street and pulled Greenblatt inside just in case the neighbors saw what was going on.

"She saw us in the parking lot!" Greenblatt continued. "You and me! So I came to get you. To get out of here. C'mon!" He acted like she should just hop in his car and drive off to Neverland.

"Why are you here Raymond?"

"It's okay. We can do it. She said it's okay! We can run away together and start an entirely new life. Away from Carol and away from Jonathan. You allow me to breathe Shanna! I have never stayed so hard for so long with anyone."

Shanna covered the baby's ears and winced. What had she done to bring this wackjob to her house?

"I feel strongly about you too," Shanna said, managing to stay calm. "But you have to go now."

"Just leave him! He's a pariah. You said so yourself." Greenblatt's eyes shined. "Come with me—we'll pack some bags! We'll move to

Havana! I'll find work. We can go out, drink wine, dance 'til dawn!"
Then Greenblatt pointed to the baby as though he'd just thought
of a great idea. "He can come too! The three of us–in Cuba."

"Are you high?"

"Little bit," Greenblatt admitted. "But that's not it. You're thinking too much. You deserve better. Our love is real. We're soul mates!
Kiss me, my love." Again Greenblatt leaned in to kiss her but this
time Shanna dodged it.

Madness, Shanna thought. She had a five-month old baby to
protect and there's a crazy man at her door she hardly knows
selling life in Cuba! She had to get him out. And quickly. She
looked at Greenblatt with his soaked beard and his wild eyes and
a boner poking through his pants and thought of the cracked
mirror he had set up for their lovemaking sessions. How he liked
to watch himself with her, and the narcissism that reflected. There
was only one way to get Greenblatt out of there and that was
through his ego.

"Listen to me very carefully," Shanna peered hypnotically into
Greenblatt's eyes. "You are without a doubt the most attractive
man I have ever laid eyes on. Handsome, masculine, brave. And
the truth, the truth is that right at this moment as I hold my baby
I am doing everything I can not to rip your clothes off and have
you take me right here in the front hall of my house. But I can't."

"Uh, why not?"

"You have no idea do you?" Shanna said, shaking her head in
bafflement. "Are you that naive?!"

"I don't think so."

"You don't know that all the nurses at the hospital want you? That
they call you 'Magic Man'? That they talk about holding a blowjob
contest in your office?!"

"They do? THEY DO?!"

"Of course they do; don't be blind! I was just the lucky one to get my hands on you first. And I thought I could hold on to you, but now I see that it's all just a schoolgirl fantasy. A man as virile as you can only withstand temptation for so long. And one woman? A joke! I mean look at me. I have a baby. I'm exhausted and I'm on my way to getting fat. You deserve someone much younger."

"I do?"

"It won't work. It's all too complicated. Elliot is my responsibility and besides I'm far too jealous."

"But I want you. I love—"

"Sure," Shanna scoffed. "For how long? I mean how long really until you get bored with me and move on to a new model? After twenty years of marriage you need your freedom."

"I-I-I—"

"Your fucking hot manly beard, that muscular chest and big old cock? Oh, I thought I could handle it. But it'll be easier if you just go now. End my heartbreak. Just go. Leave me with my empty heart and my boring life. Just fucking go!" Shanna opened the front door and shoved him out into the rain. "Go now, Magic Man!"

"What about Carol?" Greenblatt asked, rain dripping off his beard. "She took my house key."

"Find your lonely nurses. They will take you in!"

Greenblatt looked at Shanna very confused, then he thought about it and his face grew very serious. He saw it all now. Out under the rainy night sky he saw the nurses, remembered how fond of him they'd seemed lately—how flirtatious—and he saw his destiny. Yes, Shanna was right: he was a swordsman now and his fate was an all-nurse blowjob contest! "You are my only love," he told Shanna with a sincerity that was almost touching. "And I will cherish you in my heart forever!"

"Oh, do! Please do!"

Then, like a matador off to slay the bull, Greenblatt kissed Shanna one last time and marched out to his car feeling the rain beat down on his hot manly chest and pulsating ol' cock.

"Magic Man!" he said aloud and laughed–it sounded right! "To the hospital, baaaaby! To rescue those horny nurses!"

Shanna watched Greenblatt drive off, then bolt locked the door.

"What the fuck was I thinking?"

13. DELIVERY

Farb pulled into office parking just before ten p.m. He still had a good chunk of work to do before heading to the airport and would use the flight to Montreal for final tweaks. He stepped off the elevator, passed Alicia Gordon's desk and was headed into his office when a jolt of panic seized him—the lights were all on in there. If that asshole Hershorn or his cronies messed with his files as some kind of practical joke he would have to buy a gun. Instead, Farb found several neatly piled folders on his desk with a note attached: We came in today to finish. Hope you don't mind! By the way, Ferris Bueller won again!–Best, Raj Nehru (and his lesser brother, Rahul).

Farb laughed. He leafed through the files and saw everything worked out—the final budget numbers for *The Apologist* & *Canadian Eye* calculated and balanced, schedules all organized to perfection. They'd even made copies of the creative for the big meeting. Finally, everything was in place. It would just be a hand over. Farb dialed up the Brothers at home. When Rahul picked up, violent video games boomed in the background.

"I can't believe you guys," Farb said.

"Mr. Farb! We had zero to do all day. It was totally cool."

"Pack your bags, Rahul. I want you and your brother to come to Montreal."

"Wait—us? Are you sure?"

"I'm booking your flights as we speak."

Farb heard Rahul explain the situation and Raj exploded with glee.

"Hey, Rahul? I don't want to cramp your style, but try wearing something appropriate—no T-shirts, okay? Tell your brother too."

"Got it. Check that off your list. Information digested. All systems go! Wooo-hooo!"

Thank God for the Brothers. I guess karma does exist (their father would be so proud), but who knew it would come down to two grown men who still slept in a bunk bed? Farb reflected how nice it would be to give Elliot a sibling, someone he could share with and learn from. Maybe I should freeze some sperm? Farb thought about it pretty seriously.

Lights flickered on in the hallway and Sid the Security Guard performed a military salute and walked on. Farb had about six hours before he had to head to the airport. He desperately needed a nap, but the sour memory of sleeping late into his last Montreal meeting made him stay up. He fixed a pot of coffee and unearthed the video camera he'd used on a recent pilot shoot. Letters were a good way to communicate with Elliot but to really mean business a cold loving HD stare would be best–a video blog of sorts.

Farb charged up the camera and looked for a suitable place to set up the tripod. Behind his desk seemed too severe–the kid will think I'm pretentious, especially when he's a teenager. The sofa was wrong too, he shouldn't be a pushover. Standing? Farb settled on moving his desk chair into the middle of the office to put some depth in the shot. He picked up the camera, pressed "record" and was just about to set it onto the tripod when he heard a shriek and several dull thuds emanate from somewhere down the hall. Farb jumped up, camera in hand. "Hello? Hello?" The lights flickered on in the hall but no one seemed to be around. Maybe Ol' Sid had finally collapsed? The noise persisted–thuds and guttural sounds–creepily animal. Farb walked fast past Alicia Gordon's desk and followed the noise down the hall. It became more pronounced as he neared the conference room. "Sid? Are you okay over there?" Farb's heart raced as he creaked open the door.

"Sid, is that you...." What Farb saw next took his brain a good moment to process and then another to instinctively reject as if he had ingested visual poison. Perched up on the conference room table wearing only a bra and panties was Alicia Gordon. She smoked a cigarette and gazed off at a Power Point presentation entitled "Vocabulary Builder For The SAT." Next to her was a shirtless bald man crouched and grunting over several rows of cocaine. Producer's instinct made Farb steady the video camera in front of him. Alicia was saying, "So, lascivious means the same as loquacious? Or is that like, different?"

"Let me finish this rail and I'll show you," the grunting man said lasciviously.

That's when Farb coughed. The shirtless man jumped back. "Farb! What the fuck?!" It was Larson. He glistened sweat and his hairy chest was powdered white. He grabbed his shirt off the floor and tossed it at Alicia. "Jesus fucking Christ get the fuck out of here or you're fucking fired Farb!"

"Nice alliteration," Farb smirked, holding the camera steady. "The SAT committee will be impressed."

Alicia Gordon began posing seductively for Farb's camcorder, inhaling her cigarette and blowing out smoke rings. Farb just let it roll.

"Alicia, stop it goddamn it!" Larson shouted.

"Fuck that. There's finally proof I'm studying!" She arched her back provocatively and pointed to the Power Point presentation. "Loquacious."

"I said stop!"

Alicia crawled across the table cat-like and spoke directly to the camera. "Oh, no! I'm being a bad girl. Looks like I need a spanking from the big boss man Ari Larson, Executive Producer. He likes to snort coke and give SAT lessons–freak! I'm only seventeen."

Alicia smeared coke dust on her hand and held it up–Farb got a sweet close-up on that.

"Enough!" Larson raced towards the camera but Farb batted his hands away. "Farb, in my office–now!"

"Uh-oh!" Alicia giggled. "You're soooo fucking fired, Farby."

Farb lowered the camera as Alicia gave him the "call me" sign with her open hand. Shirtless, his back hair glistening, Larson lead Farb into his office and sat down in his big leather swivel chair. Typical, Farb thought as he sat–despite all arrows pointing to insanity, they were now in an official meeting, business was business, and Larson was pulling rank. "Okay Farb, here's how it's going to go down," he began. "You're going to give me the tape inside that camera and you're never going to mention this incident or your fired. Got it?"

Farb glanced down at his camera as if considering the proposal, but didn't have the chance to respond before the door swung open and Alicia Gordon, still half-naked, flung a Ziploc of coke onto Larson's lap. "Hey Farb, or whatever your name is? Whatever this piece of shit Ari says to you reverse it. I'll back your whole story. The guy even forced me to get an abortion!"

"Alicia!" Larson winced.

"Well you did, Ari! I could be prego right now. We could have a beautiful baby girl named Zola."

Larson deflated in his chair. "Okay Farb, what do you want?"

Finally, it was Farb's turn. He could have luxuriated in the moment but he decided to get right to it: "Step aside on *The Apologist* pitch."

Larson burst out laughing. "No fucking way Farb! You know Gordon would kill me if I did that."

"I can think of another reason Gordon might kill you," Farb tapped the camcorder.

"Okay, okay. You get the pitch!" Larson frowned. "I'll skip the meeting. Tell them I'm dead or something. Jesus Christ Farb what do you need this for anyway? You know what, I don't *want* to know. Now give me the fucking tape."

"Nah, I'll keep this until after the meeting. Oh, one more thing."

"I knew there'd be something."

"It has to do with a promotion."

"Look Farb I can't make you an Executive Producer. Only Gordon can do that so you might as well forget it."

"Not for me."

"A promotion that is not for you? Bullshit," Larson scoffed "Who the fuck is it for, then?"

Farb smiled.

Early the next morning The Nehru Brothers met Farb in the lobby of Place Ville Marie wearing the most absurd Gordon Gekko suits Farb had ever seen. Pin stripped shirts with big collars and gold cufflinks, bright red suspenders and gleaming Bruno Maglis.

"Nice look," Farb nodded his approval.

"We went Wall Street!" beamed Rahul. "Greed, for lack of a better word is good. Greed is right, greed works. And greed, you mark my words, will not only save *Canada's Next Great Apologist* but that other malfunctioning corporation called the Canadian Association Of Network Television! Thank you very much."

"Bravo!"

"Truncated version. Not for purists," said Raj.

The three men rode the elevator to the sixteenth floor grinning. The world was about to be theirs—all they had to do was grab it. But on the way to the conference room Farb felt that old anxiety creep in, and his knees wobbled. He stopped in front of the conference room door and held himself up as he tried not to hyperventilate.

Rahul got in his face. "Don't be nervous, Mr. Farb. You've got the gold this time." He held up the folders. "Gold!"

Farb looked at the Brothers with their trusting smiles and ridiculous outfits—they believed in him. Elliot believed him. Time he started believing in himself. Farb took a deep breath—exhaled slowly.

"Fuck it. This might be the last thing I ever do."

When Farb pushed open the conference room doors, the table of Execs (whom he had humiliated himself in front of only two weeks before) appeared before him like in some bizarre dream. Farb looked even worse than last time, paler and even more sweaty. But this time he had The Nehrus flanking him, and of course, The Gold.

"Late again Farb," Tom Hyde said, disapprovingly.

"My apologies. Traffic."

The group rolled their eyes. "And where's Larson? He was supposed to be here."

"Larson has the flu. But I'm prepared to present the materials if that works?"

"This ought to be good."

"And your associates?" asked Jen Rawlings. She sat at the head of the table, an immovable force of intimidation.

"Our newest Senior Producers, Rahul and Raj Nehru," Farb said by way of introduction. "Forgive their attire—a little hazing we do."

"No," Jen said with a sly grin. "I rather like it. The fit is nice and snug. Senior Producers, huh? So young." Jihad Jen's demeanor shifted as she checked out The Brothers. Her gaze settled on Raj, who she eyeballed like a pastry. Then she patted the seat next to her to beckoned him over. Raj complied. "So, Mr. Farb," Jen said. "What does Gordon want to go with? *Canadian Eye* or *Canada's Next Great Apologist?*"

"Well Ms. Rawlings," Farb began, his voice steady, "there comes a time when you have to wonder: does the world really need another makeover show? The Canadian people have many skills, but I think...."

"Cut the flowery talk this time, Farb," Rawlings interjected. "I had enough from Larson last time. You decided to go with *The Apologist*? Thank God. Now, the budget and outlines please?"

"Of course." Farb passed the documents down the table. "You can find summaries on page 16. I think you'll see that everything is in order."

The table of Execs opened their folders and looked things over. Farb walked them through the creative. Heads bobbed, murmurs were appreciative. One Exec said, "This is *exactly* what we've been waiting for."

"I'm thinking thirteen episodes to start," suggested Tom Hyde. "What do you think, Jen?"

But Jihad Jen was too busy flirting with Raj to even hear. She twirled a pencil coquettishly in her hair.

"Uh, Ms. Rawlings?"

"Oh! Sorry. Yes! Right, thirteen episodes. Perfect. Where do I sign? Heh-heh-hee."

Pens were wielded, signatures made and handshakes exchanged. Tom Hyde stood up. "I want to express my appreciation to Mr. Farb and his associates for their first rate work. Let's meet soon to discuss press and integration."

"Yes, good hard work," Rawlings said absently, then dipped her hand under the table and squeezed Raj's knee.

As the Execs shuffled out, Rahul stood next to Farb watching his brother and Jihad Jen in awe. "Always the bridesmaid, never the bride," he said.

"Oh, your day will come Rahul."

"Share a cab back to the airport?" said Rahul.

"You go ahead—I've got some loose ends to tie up."

"Okay boss–see you back."

"Enjoy the trip, Mr. Senior Producer."

Rahul smiled widely, saluted Farb military-style then bounced out. Farb gathered the documents and walked outside to hail a cab.

"Car dealership," Farb told the driver. "Deluxe, *s'il vous plait.*"

Farb cruised the streets of Montreal in his newly leased Boxster. Sherbrooke, then St. Laurent and, then the park beneath Mount Royal's illuminated cross. Toronto would have turned Mount Royal into a theme park if given the chance: ten bucks admission, café lattes at the summit. He parked near the residences of McGill University and walked around. How tiny. Even early in the afternoon Nirvana blasted and guys got rowdy on Fin Du Monde. Same music, same beer. One kid with his face painted red leaned out his window and yelled to Farb: "If you're looking for your daughter she's not here!" Laughter all around. So Farb was the old guy now? A minute ago he was them. Crazy.

Campus hadn't changed either–the old austere gray buildings, prim patches of grass, bike racks, pretensions. As Farb walked past Redpath Library a flashback stopped him cold. It was the day he secured a key internship at a local TV station. He was strolling the campus feeling great when he spotted a beautiful girl with long curly hair and a swan-like neck all dressed in black. She sat on the library steps and struggled to light a cigarette from the wrong end.

"I wouldn't do that if I were you," Farb said to the girl.

Shanna eyed him skeptically–she was wearing eighties punk black eye makeup and a ripped D.O.A. T-shirt with safety pins–he was in pleated slacks and a frat boy polo. "You the campus police I keep hearing about?" she said, bored. "I can smoke wherever the fuck I want."

"It's a free campus," Farb replied, "but you're lighting that cigarette from the wrong end, and I just wouldn't do that if I were you."

Shanna looked down—the cigarette had begun to char and sizzle at the filter.

"If I may?" Farb stepped forward, plucked a new cigarette from her pack, lit it and passed it to her. "See that yellow part here, that's the filter. You can suck on that."

"I'll decide what I suck on, thank you very much," Shanna snapped. "I was just too tired to notice. Up all night at Fouf."

"Sounds pretty wild."

"It was. It is. It's like my life."

Shanna inhaled and coughed violently—Farb laughed and that pissed Shanna off—this square guy teasing her, and for some reason she couldn't come up with an edgy fuck-off line she did with all the other jerks. "Thanks, I can deal with things from here."

"Oh, you've made that abundantly clear," said Farb. "I'm just worried about everyone else. The way you look you may start a trend—or a fire. Soon the whole campus will be lighting cigarettes backwards."

"The way I look?"

Farb looked at her very seriously, there was almost pain in his eyes. "You have the most beautiful smile."

Shanna burst out laughing and blew smoke all in Farb's face. She looked him over suspiciously and grinned. "How old are you anyway?"

It was their purest moment. Farb wished he could freeze it in time, go back to Shanna's first laugh on the steps of Redpath Library and drink it in. But he could never go back. Time fizzled away and there was nothing left of it—nothing to apologize for and much less to forgive. There was only to act. Elliot taught him that. So Farb picked up his pace and headed back to the car. He had one last thing to get done.

14. VENGEANCE

On the previous rainy night in Toronto, when Farb pulled out of his driveway with his windshield wipers on but his headlights off, Carol Greenblatt drove along the same street also with headlights down. She'd found Shanna Farb's address in her husband's blue choir binder under "Contacts" and was on her way to pay her a visit when Farb's car narrowly avoided hitting her. Farb drove on, unaware of the near collision, and Carol swerved to the side of the road. When she stopped it was directly across the street from the address she'd scribbled down.

"Jerkoff!"

Carol looked out the window at Shanna's house. It was the kind of quaint, neat place that she and Ray always dreamed of moving to. Carol was impressed by the well-manicured lawn and colorful garden. Despite herself she wondered if Shanna did the gardening herself, and decided that should they get beyond their conflict over this mess their mutual love of gardening would be a good place to start a friendship.

A car turned the corner and blinded Carol with its headlights. By instinct she shut off her ignition and sloped down in her seat. She didn't want to be caught snooping or have the police called on her as a suspicious character. It would be an embarrassing situation to explain. But the car that pulled past her and right into the driveway of Shanna Farb's house was too familiar for a second look—even through the downpour of rain she could see it was her husband Raymond. Carol watched the selfish scumbag park right in her driveway as if he lived there, and with a newspaper flagging over his head, run to the front door. He stood there in the rain for a while getting soaked and Carol felt a misplaced instinct to run out and bring him an umbrella. But the door opened and there was Shanna Farb, wearing a bathrobe and cradling a baby in her arms. Carol watched her husband move into the doorway and kiss Shanna, then the door shut behind them.

"So he's already moved in! Son of a bitch!"

Carol gunned the engine and drove off almost hoping they'd hear the screech of her tires and get spooked. But it would have been a hollow warning. Because had Carol waited outside Shanna Farb's house for only a few extra minutes she would have seen the door open again and her shithead husband run back to his car, rejected. She would have watched him flip on an oldies station, snarl like Elvis, and drive off to the hospital where he intended to initiate a sex orgy with dozens of steaming hot nympho nurses. But she didn't. Carol only saw Raymond enter the house and kiss Shanna, and she accept him in. Into her lovely little home, with its well-maintained garden and her bottle-fed baby. Just like that. A new life for Raymond, and for Carol nothing at all. As she drove along the dark streets Carol plotted revenge. They could have their new life but would have to suffer the consequences of her vengeance.

That night Carol fell into bed and immediately to sleep. To her surprise it was a deep and dreamless sleep, one that had the power to quell old grudges, give optimism to a new day. But it didn't. Carol woke the next morning to find the focus of her anger sharpened and her imagination running wild. She pictured the two of them, right at that moment lying in bed maybe making love a second time on her six hundred thread count Egyptian combed cotton sheets. Or worse sitting around her bright kitchen table smiling as they fed the baby breakfast. A whole new life. Greenblatt had never been a particularly attentive father to their two daughters—he escaped much of the mundane responsibilities of parenthood because he was a doctor, and if ever there was a real emergency in the house, he would know what to do. It was an insurance policy that Carol paid into endlessly. But aside from Beth cutting her finger on a shattered vase when she was nine, requiring only a few stitches, her husband's big heroic moment never came. And now that it never would, Carol saw that far from some secular saint her husband was just some schmuck who stared at vaginas all day, scoping out the best for a possible affair. And look at her now. All alone, haggard from all her giving, with a cellulite ass and a roadmap of wrinkles leading to nowhere–that son of a bitch!

Carol opened the bedroom windows. Another dreary, rainy day–a heavy day. She walked to the dresser and retrieved Raymond's pistol from its velvet case. She kept it there overnight for self-defense–crime had risen in the area and she might need to protect herself. But as she paced the bedroom feeling the heft of the gun Carol wondered if self-defense was really her motivation? She stood before a full-length mirror and held the gun to her temple. How would this feel, you selfish prick? She could leave a note, there would be a big mess to clean up, all his associates at the hospital would know that he did this. A blood stain on his happy new life! Carol looked at herself seriously, gun to her big fat head and scoffed. "How unoriginal can you get, Carol? That's sooo what you would do!" She could already read the headlines: Scorned housewife lives the life of a victim then kills herself so her husband can live an untangled life with a younger woman. Tombstone inscription. Pathetic. In truth he'd be glad to have her out of the way. The girls would lean on him for support and he could use his professional opinion to paint her as unbalanced, but what a shame. That wasn't revenge it was submission! No. She wasn't going to be Raymond's little victim anymore. She wasn't going to be stepped on or pushed out of the way. She needed her revenge; not necessarily violent revenge although she yearned to injure him. Revenge by humiliation. To reveal Raymond as the weasel he was right in front of Shanna Farb and watch him cower, literally bearded in fear! If Shanna could see with her own eyes that he would use her baby as a shield before taking a bullet himself, then she would have no choice but to leave him. Carol knew that in a way Shanna was under the same spell she had been under–Raymond was a doctor and so he wielded power, was indeed a hero. In reality he was nothing of the sort. Shanna would soon realize this. The spell would be broken and she would leave him as easily as he had left her. Carol simply needed to scare the daylights out of her husband, scare them both to death, and let Shanna Farb see what a weakling of a man she had invited into her home.

Carol leafed through the yellow pages and dialed a number under Handyman.

"Hi, Jim? Yes, this is Carol Greenblatt on Orchard Drive. Yes, you once got my door open when I locked myself out. Well you're not going to believe this but I seemed to have done it again! Is there some way you could come over and show me how to break in? I promise not to tell the police. Ha! Great. When can I expect you? It's pouring out here."

15. TOGETHER

Farb sped along the 401 to Toronto as the evening sky turned black and blue. Cold drizzle forced him to pull up the roof of his Boxster but still he enjoyed the smooth luxury ride. With all systems go on *The Apologist,* Farb's Creator fee was a lock and, aside from the sum he'd dropped on leasing the car, that money would be tucked away in Trust for Elliot. Whatever Farb found when he got home, a man in his bed, divorce papers served, Elliot's future would be secure. A calmness washed over him at the idea of it. He knew the feeling would fade but he was learning to savor it, and that might be the best he could hope for in this life. Still, there was one thing left to do—a long-overdue call. He pulled off at a gas station and fed the payphone.

"Glad to hear you've changed your mind," said Dr. Arupal. "You'll be happy to hear we have in a new approach in from Boston—not quite experimental but it's pretty revolutionary for us, and I know you'll be impressed since it's from the wonderful America you're so impressed with. We can start your prep first thing in the morning."

"I'm in," said Farb.

"It's not going to be an easy road," Dr. Arupal reminded him. "I know you understand there are significant risks, but we have the best…"

"… best medical staff in Toronto?"

"I was going to say that you will be looked after. And that you are doing the right thing. And that you are brave."

"Sure doesn't feel that way, Doctor."

"You'll see. Goodnight Mr. Farb—see you bright and early."

Farb got back in his car. He rolled down his windows and as he merged back onto the highway he yelled out: "I'M GOING TO

LIVE!" Cars honked all around him. "DO YOU HEAR ME?! I'M GOING TO LIVE! I'M GOING TO BE ABLE TO TASTE LIFE! I'M GOING TO SEE MY SON GROW UP! I'M GOING TO FIND OUT WHAT HAPPENS IN *MAD MEN*!"

It was past midnight when Farb got home. The lights were off so he tiptoed upstairs so as not to wake Shanna. In the baby's room Farb laid down his coat and pulled the baby out of the crib and into his arms. Elliot was wearing powder blue pajamas and his black tufts of hair smelled sweetly of shampoo. His little lips puckered as he breathed heavily–maybe he was dreaming?

"We're going to make it," Farb whispered, kissing Elliot on his cheeks. "Dad's going to be sick but we're going to make it. I promise. Sweet, sweet baby boy."

Farb closed his eyes and rocked the baby gently against his chest. This was it, his happiest moment, frozen in time.

"Jonathan?" Shanna whispered from the darkness. "Is that you?"

Farb tucked Elliot back into the crib, kissed him one last time and entered the bedroom. "Hey." As soon as Farb saw Shanna's face with her trails of tears and hair everywhere he knew she'd figured things out.

"It's over with him," she said, staring at her hands.

"That's good."

"I was stupid. But you should have told me, Jonathan. I could have helped. I could have been there. I-I-I could have...."

Farb sat on the edge of the bed and put a hand on Shanna's cheek. "Things are going to be harder now. You'll be alone a lot. Elliot will be a challenge."

"I can do it. I want to. I'm not going anywhere."

"He's an amazing kid, Shanna. He's growing up and he's going to be great."

"I know."

"He's got a real chance to be happy."

They held each other for a while and Shanna sobbed into Farb's chest.

When Farb finally got to sleep it was dead still and dreamless. He slept like a man who'd gotten hard work done and could finally rest. He slept like a man of action. He slept just like a baby.

16. THRIVE

At precisely 3:03 a.m. that night–per the police report–after the lights were out at the Farb residence and the Farbs were fast asleep, a car pulled up next to the driveway with its headlights off. Mrs. Carol Greenblatt, recently abandoned by her husband Raymond and convinced that he was living at the Farb residence, approached the side of the house with a crowbar and pried the door open. She needed little help since the door was left unlocked, but there was indeed forced entry. Mrs. Greenblatt hid the crowbar in a nearby rose bush and entered the house. She wielded a loaded World War II-era pistol from her husband's collection (Karbinger-S43) and climbed the stairs. According to her confession (#F45097GH) Mrs. Greenblatt was in search of her husband, who she claimed she only wanted to scare with the gun. Instead, she walked into the room of the Farb's five-month-old son Elliot, who was sleeping soundly. Time estimates state that Mrs. Greenblatt was in the baby's room for several minutes "standing over the crib and watching the baby sleep," when Jonathan Farb, awoken perhaps by a rustling down the hall, walked in and encountered the assailant. A confrontation ensued in which the assailant drew the gun. (NOTE: According to Mrs. Greenblatt's confession she recognized Mr. Farb from the local synagogue). Mr. Farb's attempt to calm Mrs. Greenblatt failed. Two shots were fired, one into the Farb's left shoulder the other grazing the top of his skull. The assailant then fled the scene of the crime (approx. 3:18 a.m.), and later at 5:06 a.m. turned herself into local police.

Thus read the police file that was distributed to the court on the day of Carol Greenblatt's arraignment. But the truth–as often is the case–was far more complicated. In fact Jonathan Farb did not wake up as described in the police report from a noise down the hall. He had set his alarm for 3:06 a.m. and just happened to be checking on the baby when he stumbled into Carol Greenblatt and her gun. Farb's plan was to wake up early enough to take his son on a short fishing excursion before dawn. He was scheduled to show up at North York General at 10 a.m. for treatment of a tumor and figured that he could get in some good father-son bonding before he had to check in. Farb's intended lesson plan was on the subject of Manhood, the final lesson on his list, and a fishing pond would set the scene. Farb wrote a note for Shanna (which she later hid from the police in fear they would take her husband for the whack job and not Carol Greenblatt), got dressed and walked out of the bedroom. When Farb discovered Carol Greenblatt, a matronly woman in her fifties peering over Elliot's crib, it was with a kind of confused casualness that came with lack of sleep. Farb had been home so infrequently lately that he almost took the woman for a babysitter that Shanna had hired without letting him know.

"Hey there," Farb said simply.

It wasn't until the hall light illuminated the woman's eyes that Farb saw something shifty, red and unbalanced. And then he saw the gun.

"They took everything from me—my whole life," Carol sobbed, waving the pistol absently.

Farb quickly realized that this must be the other cuckold. "We can fix this," he said, palms wide open. "We can fix them. Just put down the gun, okay? We'll do it together."

"But how can you be with her?" Carol cried, her face red and lined with tears. "In bed with that slut!" The baby began to moan awake. Carol lifted the gun to her cheek and wiped away tears.

"No one has to know about this—just put it down."

Shanna's voice called out from the bedroom. "Jonathan? Who are you talking to? Is there someone there?"

And it was then that Carol's eyes became demented and she raised the gun level to Farb. "She's in there, isn't she? Is he in there too?! I'll kill him! I'll just kill him!"

"It's just her," Farb said. "And me. He's not here. We're all alone."

Carol looked Farb over. So pale and sickly but with a kindness in his eyes–like her, he had some understanding of life's pain. She wouldn't harm him. But she couldn't let her get away with this. She needed to satisfy her vengeance, to teach them both a lesson and make it impossible for Shanna to look at Raymond without contempt. For his selfishness, for his cowardice and deceit. There was only one solution. Carol took a step back and pointed the gun at Elliot's crib. Time froze. Farb lunged forward and let out a cry as colorful sparks ignited in his eyes. The first bullet shattered the bones in his shoulder, sending shockwaves of pain to his brain and hot wet blood gushing down his back. He caught Carol's arm and despite his injury, held on, feeling strong enough to overpower her, to get her away from Elliot when a slip caused another explosion and the sound was unbelievable and the light brilliant, illuminating the room for a millisecond so that Farb could see Carol and her wild and terrified eyes. He heard Shanna screeching and under it Elliot's wail as the gun dropped to the floor and Carol went running out of the room and down the stairs and the blur and the ringing and the blasts of light and color and sound and scattershots of pain and numbness around Farb as the world spun and Shanna screamed.

"Jonathan! Jonathan!" until her voice went hoarse and Farb was in her arms with all his blood and shattered bones, and before he lost consciousness Farb was allowed another millisecond to compose his final thoughts and he focused on the sweet music of Elliot's living wail "Waaaaa-haaaa!" so strong and vibrant–the kid *did* have healthy lungs, didn't he? Could be the next Pavarotti! A star for sure but beyond that... he was going to live–his boy was going to live! His boy who is so loved will grow up and grow tall and be a man–and as the sirens came screaming, and Shanna let go of Farb and he felt a tugging at his legs and neck from the EMT, a calmness spread over him like he'd never felt before and he was able to imagine himself out there at the fishing pond with Elliot, reciting the lesson he hoped to teach him as they cast off their first line. He would tell Elliot to keep looking at things with astonishment and wonder–to fill each day with light and not fear and for god sakes don't worry so much because everything is already written just like it's supposed to be and fate is something real and Elliot your fate is good and I am proud, so proud of you, and so thankful that your story had been written so beautifully and that the world had afforded you the opportunity to thrive.

17. FAREWELL

Snow drifted along the parking lot at Temple Beth-El. A walking path was shoveled and salted, but the bitter wind whipped more snow onto the path, leaving slippery patches of covered ice for the congregants to navigate. Due to construction to expand the synagogue, cars had parked next to the Rabbi's new library (another recent addition), but that meant a short walk along the edges of the frozen ravine. Rabbi Klotz nodded mournfully as he welcomed congregants into the synagogue, pointing them to a room where they could remove their coats and scarves and boots. Klotz had gone gray over the years, his glasses were thicker and his belt looser—he was a man who'd indulged in his fair share of Bar Mitzvah buffets; but he'd also mastered the art of hospitality and the synagogue, although bigger now, was still a place where Jews could walk around in socks.

Dozens of mourners wearing solemn faces and dark suits entered the main sanctuary and took their seats. The attendance was decidedly for a man who was well liked, but close to too few in his lifetime. The Cantor sang a mournful prayer signaling that the service was to begin. Several rows back sat Rahul and Raj Nehru, both graying around the temples too, although looking distinguished in their expensive suits. Raj sat next to his ten year old daughter and Jen Rawlings-Nehru, who was still Jihad Jen to those who feared her. Also seated were several members of Farb's family and Shanna's elderly mother and father. Also there was George, who sat in the audience as well, a man now well into his forties. He had found a partner, a lovely cherubic woman who wore two coats—they squeezed each other's hands as the Cantor sang. The rest of the congregants were an assemblage of TV producers, Network suits, and a smattering of nurses and other care providers who knew Farb only in his deteriorated state.

"So sorry for your loss," one of them said to Shanna, shaking her hand. "He was a fighter. Right up to the end."

Shanna smiled sweetly and nodded. Looking every bit her age, Shanna's eyes were wrinkled and heavy and her hair once so long and black had been cut short and left to gray at the roots. But Shanna's mouth, which had spent many of the last years advocating for her husband's health but also singing as a stand-in for the Cantor in the choir, had been spared the ravages of time. Her lips were soft and pliable, a place where her youth lived on.

"We should sit now, Mom." Elliot placed a gentle hand on Shanna's shoulder. A lanky fifteen years old, he was still awkwardly thin for his suit, his neck stuck out like a celery stick and touches of teenage angst manifested in long shaggy black hair that fell over his forehead. In appearance he had inherited much from Shanna, but his long face and dark intense eyes (always scanning, always looking for vultures), that was all Farb. Shanna knew Elliot as a thoughtful and intelligent boy and though she worried about his prospects for happiness in life, she also recognized in him a quiet confidence that would lead him to do whatever he wanted regardless of peer pressure.

The Cantor cued the choir and they opened their blue binders. Shanna winced when for a split second she thought she saw Greenblatt. But no, it was a new bearded man who had taken his place. An illusion, a sour memory from years back.

The Rabbi led the Mourner's Kaddish then delivered his sermon, careful to remind the congregants that some of the additions to the synagogue had come as a result of the deceased's philanthropy. "A man whose spirit lives on in the hearts of his loved ones and in the halls of Temple Beth-El." The Rabbi then called on anyone who wanted to say a few words. Elliot squeezed his mother's hand and walked to the *bema*. He unfolded several pieces of paper, looked out to the faces in the congregation, and seeing that Shanna was already tearing up with pride, Elliot gave her an exasperated look as if to say "Mom, relax!" Then he began.

"A lot of people my age love to complain about their parents," said Elliot. "They say they're suffocating. Or they complain they're never around. Out working. On business trips. I'm not above complaining either, believe me, but I never understood why so much anger was focused on the people who supposedly love you most. My mother–sorry Mom–can definitely be accused of being a bit suffocating, and my dad, workaholic that he was, skipped his share of family dinners. I grew up getting to know my dad after he survived a bout with a brain tumor and a violent attack that came very close to ending his life and mine had he not intervened. Dad tried to make up for his long recovery with a growing career and a family life that he did his best to provide attention to. He fought a benign tumor, and when, incredibly, a new malignant tumor appeared three years ago he had the clarity to say that it reminded him of how lucky he was to survive a decade before."

"Everyone told me what a shame it was that he was sick. They told me stories about how energetic and how combative he used to be–some described him as annoyingly full of life. What a shame it was for me not to have that dad to throw around the baseball in the park with, or to help me with math homework. Everyone wanted to know if I wanted to talk about this problem. I was sent to therapists who urged me to get in touch with my anger and loneliness. I confess I was angry for a while. But I was never lonely. Because Dad was always there, albeit mostly in a hospital bed. When things were crazy at school or just in life in the past few years he was there–I could count on him. I got to know him about as well as you can know anyone, and he knew me too."

"Back when I was only a few months old and my dad was ill the first time, he wrote me a pile of letters that are very special to me now. My mom keeps telling me he wasn't all there when he wrote them, that he was acting strangely before he went to the hospital for his first treatment, but I think he wrote his truth. Imagine, you're probably going to die and you take time to write letters to someone who can't even read yet? I'd probably spend my last days chasing girls–sorry mom. But knowing he might die, he took the time to make sure that I knew what kind of life he wanted for me. It was a life without fear, a life of action and consequence. A life that he couldn't afford but tried to afford for me."

"I've read a lot of wacked out books lately–look, I'm a teenager. And while it's hard to put my dad's letters in the genre of experimental fiction, for a guy who was supposed to be a sell-out Reality TV Producer, Dad missed his calling. He had a way of predicting the future, and though he missed the mark on a whole bunch of stuff (sorry Dad I won't be going to McGill Business School and I'm not dating a cheerleader), on a few things he was right on. For one thing I'm not sure how he could have known I'd be so into writing. It's a secret I hid even from him, and hey maybe I'm just a cliché teenager, but still! He knew me before I even grew up."

"Of all the letters this one's my favorite. It's a foreword he wrote for what will be my first published book of poetry someday. But before I read it I want to sign off the way my dad ended so many of his letters to me. Dad, wherever you are, I love you too, and I miss you. *Carpe Tuchus!*"

Jeff Oliver is a programming executive at the Food Network and has worked as a producer on shows including *Last Comic Standing, Big Brother,* and the very uncomplicated *Denise Richards: It's Complicated.* A graduate of McGill University and Brooklyn College's MFA in Fiction, his stories have appeared in *The Nerve Magazine, Yankee Pot Roast,* and *The Brooklyn Review.* He was born in Toronto and lives in Maplewood, New Jersey, with his wife Liz and son Evan."